D1093678

Voyage to Tasmania

Voyage to Tasmania

Richard Parker

Illustrated by Prudence Seward

THE **BOBBS-MERRILL** COMPANY, INC.
A SUBSIDIARY OF HOWARD W. SAMS & CO., INC.
Publishers • INDIANAPOLIS • NEW YORK

Library of Congress Catalog Card Number 63-11660
Text Copyright © 1961 Richard Parker
Illustrations Copyright © 1961 Brockhampton Press, Ltd.
Printed in the United States of America
All Rights Reserved
First Edition

Contents

230770

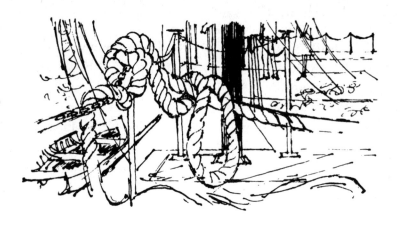

1. The unwilling passenger

Ray Manser hung over the rail on C deck and scowled at the gray customs shed, the wet dock with its puddles and untidy litter of ropes, steel hawsers, baggage and hurrying people. He wished he were still at home, sitting by a warm fire with the curtains drawn against the miserable February weather, and hot crumpets just being put on the table for tea. Then he remembered for the hundredth time that he did not have a home any more. He scowled again and for a moment his view of the dock was blurred; he had to blink hard two or three times to make it come clear again.

"Oh, there you are, then!" said Mrs. Wiley, coming halfway across the deck toward him. "Why don't you come down, Ray, and have a look at the cabin? It's quite nice down there."

Ray shook his head. "I want to be here when we sail," he said.

"But that's not for three hours yet," said Mrs. Wiley. "And besides, it's so cold up here. You'll get a chill or something. The steward said they'd be serving a late tea for the children soon, and I'm sure you must be hungry after the long day we've had."

"I'd rather stay up here, Mrs. Wiley, really I would," Ray said. He began to press his top lip gingerly with his fingers, feeling the pain in his gums where two of his top teeth had been knocked out in the accident more than two months before.

Mrs. Wiley looked worried. "Surely those old gums aren't still hurting you?" she said. "I keep thinking there might be a bit of root left there. Maybe we ought to have had an X-ray after all."

"No. I'm all right," said Ray abruptly, and turned back to stare at the dockside. Mrs. Wiley stood for a while, not at all sure what to do, and then went below. In the cabin she and her daughter had on H deck she said, "I'm worried about that young Ray. I know it's natural for him to be miserable, after all he's gone through, but he does seem to be giving way to it. He just won't come away from the rail, and there's nothing to see except the rain and that dreary wet shed."

"If it's natural for him to be miserable, why worry?" said Ila, who was sixteen and not very interested in sad eleven-year-old boys. "He'll get over it when we sail. There'll be too much to interest him. He can't go on brooding forever."

Up on deck Ray went on brooding, though. When he pressed the back of his hand against his lip the pain in his gums came again, and when he felt that, he remembered everything very clearly—the cold, crisp morning in November and the car ride to Tenterden to fetch the puppy he had been promised for his birthday. He remembered the feeling he'd had, half-excited, half-hungry because he'd not eaten much breakfast, leaning forward in the back seat of the car with his head poked forward between his father and his mother.

"Are you sure it'll be all right to take him away from his mother?" he had asked, for at least the sixth time. "Is seven weeks old enough? Won't he be miserable?"

And before his father could answer, the truck had swung round the corner at them. There was one dreadful moment when Ray had had time to see that it was a farm truck with sheep loaded in two layers.

And he had thought to himself quite clearly, "Nothing can happen to us today, though, because it's my birthday."

But it had happened all the same, and now he was on a ship just about to sail halfway round the world to take him to an aunt he had never even seen, living in a strange city he had never even heard of before, called Hobart, in Tasmania. At the thought of it he pressed his mouth so hard that he almost cried out aloud with the pain.

Something prodded him sharply in the back and he turned to see a boy of about his own age standing just behind him, smiling self-confidently. "What's up with you?" he said. "You look as if you were just going to burst into tears."

"Mind your own business," said Ray angrily.

The boy did not seem put out. He did not even stop smiling. He was a large boy and smiling came naturally to him. He was not fat, but smooth like a seal, and very nearly the same shape, having a thick neck and sloping shoulders. "My name's Andrew Newman," he said. "My mother and I are emigrating to Australia. My dad went last year and now we're going out to him. He's in Sydney and he's making a lot of money so we shall be rich when we get there."

"That's very interesting," said Ray sarcastically.

He had taken an instant and absolute dislike to this boy; he was altogether too full of himself.

From the loudspeakers came the sound of a bugle. "I bet you don't know what that means," said Andrew.

Ray did not know but he could not bring himself to admit it. He turned back to the rail and leaned over it again.

"I know," said Andrew. "It means there's a meal down in the salon. Good, eh? Coming down?"

"No," said Ray.

"I am. I'm pretty hungry, actually."

"I hope you make yourself sick."

11

"Do you mean seasick?" asked Andrew. "I'm never seasick. Well, cheerio. See you around, I expect."

Ray did not answer and at last the boy went away.

A couple of sailors behind him had been dragging the sailcloth off a large hatch next to the empty swimming pool. Now one of them came over to him. Ray noticed first of all the oily clothes and dirty arms, then the black beard, and finally the young face and friendly eyes. "We're going to start slinging cases into this hatchway now," he said. "Just in the line of fire, where you're standing, young man . . ."

"If you want me to move," said Ray, "why not just say so?"

The sailor looked hurt and moved away without saying any more. Ray went on standing where he was for a while out of sheer stubbornness, but then, as it obviously was dangerous with nets stuffed with cases and trunks swinging up and over his head, he wandered slowly away with his hands stuffed in his pockets. He looked into the empty swimming pool. and thought how small it seemed—hardly room for one person to swim decently let alone a whole ship full. He found the central staircase and went down slowly, staring at himself in the huge mirror on the wall halfway down. The clock set in the mirror showed twenty minutes past five.

The deck below was D deck and it was almost

deserted. This deck was enclosed by a glass partition. There were piles of folding chairs roped together, and cane chairs stacked on tables away in one
corner. On one side of the deck there was a great
jumbled pile of baggage around which half a dozen
white-coated stewards were working, picking out a
case here and a case there and carrying them off.
Ray saw a leather suitcase that looked like Mrs.
Wiley's, but he wasn't interested enough to look
closer and make sure. He wandered on along the
deck until he came to a door marked, in large printed
letters, CABIN CLASS. The door was open so Ray
walked through, although he knew perfectly well he
had no right to.

Beyond was a corridor with people hurrying backward and forward along it and popping in and out
of cabin doors. A steward went by carrying cases, followed by a lady in a fur coat. Ray went on along the
passage, trying to look as if he knew where he was
going.

Suddenly he came to a large open space, a sort of
central hallway, with wide stairs going up and down,
and all sorts of offices with people at counters writing or talking. The floor of the hall was decorated
with a large mosaic picture of an Indian's head,
feather headdress and all. Ray stopped, not sure
which way to go next. He felt lost and was afraid

someone would come up to him and tell him to go back to the end of the ship where he belonged. To hide his nervousness he frowned fiercely and stared at the people around as if he were a detective looking for a criminal.

Then he noticed that one side of the hall was open and led into the covered mouth of a gangway which in turn led straight down on to the dock. Well, why not? he thought to himself. Why not make a bolt for it? Mrs. Wiley would never guess where he was and wouldn't find out until after the ship had sailed. No one else would worry about him because all his friends thought he was on the way to Australia. To be on the safe side he could change his name.

Ray edged toward the gangway until he was standing almost next to the officer whose job seemed to consist of looking at people's papers as they came on board and calling a steward to show them to their cabins. Soon a foreign gentleman came up the gangway. He had two cameras slung over one shoulder, a pair of binoculars in a case over the other, a portable typewriter in his left hand, a heavy suitcase in his right, and a briefcase tucked under his arm. He did not immediately understand what the officer said to him and began to put down his cases and search through all his pockets for his passport.

"No, sir, not your passport," said the officer. "May

I see your sailing ticket because it has the cabin number on it? Or perhaps you can remember your cabin number?"

The foreign gentleman put away his passport and opened his briefcase.

"Perhaps you would tell me your name, sir," cried the officer, and began to flick over the sheets of the passenger list.

Ray decided it was the moment he was waiting for and slipped behind the officer on to the gangway; the officer was much too busy to notice him. As it happened the gangway was quite empty. Ray saw the empty slope in front of him and was suddenly tempted to make a dash for it. He controlled himself, however, and sauntered down, hoping he looked as if he had just seen someone off and was now going ashore in the ordinary way. He wished he had not let Mrs. Wiley take his overcoat down to the cabin; he certainly could not go back for it now.

When he was two-thirds of the way down the gangway someone came on it from the lower end. Ray kept his eyes down and squeezed over to one side to leave room. The footsteps came up quickly as if the person were in a hurry. Then they stopped.

"You're a long way off course," said a familiar voice.

Ray looked up to see the bearded sailor, no longer

grimy, but dapper and neat with gleaming white square-necked shirt. He didn't know what to say, so he kept silent.

"Tag along and I'll soon show you the way," said the sailor and went past Ray and on up the gangway. There didn't seem to be any sensible alternative, so Ray turned and followed him, past the officer still dealing with the foreign gentleman, back along the corridor and through the door marked CABIN CLASS. This the sailor closed behind them.

"Here," exclaimed the sailor. "I bet you missed your tea. They were going to serve it at five, and you were up on deck then."

"I didn't want anything," Ray said.

"You will, though," said the sailor. "There's nothing else till breakfast. And you never want to go to sea on an empty stomach."

The Unwilling Passenger

Ray shrugged his shoulders. "If it's too late I shall have to put up with it, won't I?"

"Independent type, eh?" said the sailor with a smile. "Well, there's something to be said for it. All the same, I think we could wangle a little something. Could you manage a slice of cake and a mug of tea, for instance?"

Ray was torn two ways at once; he didn't want anyone to do him favors, and on the other hand he did feel quite hungry. Hunger won. "Well, I might . . ." he said, though not very graciously.

"Keep coming then," said the sailor, and led the way to the very end of the deck and through a door marked CHILDREN'S PLAYROOM. Behind this was a very narrow passage and in the side of the passage a small door. The sailor opened this door.

"One of my hiding places," he said. It was very small, almost a cupboard. "Take a seat!"

In fact, apart from a large ball of twine and an upturned empty paint tin there was nothing to sit on. Ray sat on the ball of twine judging it to be softer, and stared round. It was a sort of storeroom with shelves carrying paint, brushes, rope, wire, tools, odd lengths of wood and a real scramble of bits and pieces. The sailor squatted on the paint tin and dragged out from a corner a tin box that originally contained cookies and an immense thermos flask

17

that must have held at least half a gallon of liquid.

"Handy things, these," he said as he unscrewed the top of the thermos. "I got this in Aden on the last trip. Fill them up in the galley and they hold enough to last all night. Currant or seed?"

This meant cake. Ray chose currant and was handed a slice so thick that he could only just get the corner into his mouth. He held the cake in one hand and a mug of hot tea in the other, and for the first time that day he felt almost cheerful.

"Now," said the sailor. "I'm Arthur Dobbs. Who are you?"

2. S. S. *Huron* puts to sea

In ten minutes, under the influence of the tea and the currant cake, Ray was telling this friendly sailor things about himself that he had been keeping hidden inside for weeks. He told Arthur about the accident in which his mother and father had been killed, and about how he had been in the hospital himself for nearly two weeks.

"And I had these two front teeth knocked crooked," he said. "They had to take them out in the end because they couldn't be fixed."

"What about your relatives?" Arthur asked. "Aunts and uncles and all that?"

Ray scowled as if remembering something unpleasant. "My Aunt Alice used to come and see me in the hospital," he said. "But she didn't want to have me living with her. All she kept talking about was what a good time the kids had in one of these Homes. She was just trying to get me used to the idea. But Mrs. Wiley—she lived right next door to us—wouldn't have it and she kept having rows with Aunt Alice. She said it wasn't right I should be sent to an orphanage when I had relatives who could look after me."

"I was brought up in an orphanage," Arthur said. "It wasn't as bad as all that."

"Oh," said Ray, and wasn't sure how to go on. "Anyway Mrs. Wiley said she would have taken care of me herself only she and Ila, that's her daughter, were going back to Australia. And then she found out that my father's sister Netta was living in Tasmania, so she wrote lots of letters and in the end Aunt Netta said I was to go out there and live with her, and Mrs. Wiley was to bring me when she sailed. And that's why I'm here now."

"This Mrs. Wiley sounds nice," said Arthur.

"Oh, she's all right," said Ray grudgingly. "She's English anyway. But Ila was born in Australia; I can't get on with her. She talks funny for one thing. She says things are crook when she means they're wrong, and she called fields 'paddocks,' and if I put grease on my hair she says I look like a bodgie, and she keeps saying 'Good on yer' all the time. I mean it's silly the way she talks."

Arthur unscrewed his immense thermos and poured two more mugs of tea. "You'll get used to that when you've been at school a couple of weeks," he said.

"But I don't want to get used to it. I don't even want to go," said Ray stubbornly. "Nobody really wants me. I'm just a nuisance to them. I don't like being a charity case. I don't want people running around fixing things up for me because they think they ought to. I don't want to go to Australia. I just want to go back to the way things always were, with Mum and Dad, and . . ."

He stopped suddenly because he knew if he said another word he would start to cry. To cover his silliness he took a huge gulp of tea, which turned out to be very hot and set him spluttering and coughing. After that any tears that did happen to be in his eyes seemed to have got there as a result of the tea.

"Well," said Arthur, "it's all right for you, but I've got to show myself around the deck in case someone gets the idea I'm not doing my job. Can you find your own way down to your cabin?"

Ray went off, feeling on the whole a good deal better for getting his troubles off his chest. After getting lost a couple of times he found himself down on H deck and also found Mrs. Wiley's cabin. He recognized her coat on the back of the door and Ila's handbag on one of the beds. There was no sign of his things, however, and he was just beginning to feel lost again when a steward came to the door and asked him if his name was Ray.

"Your mum asked me to keep an eye on you," he said.

"Mrs. Wiley's not my mother," said Ray.

"Well, your aunt then."

"Nor my aunt. She isn't any relation."

"All right," said the steward with a grin. "That's not the point anyway. Come on and I'll show you your cabin."

"Aren't I going to be in here?"

"A big boy like you sleeping in a ladies' cabin!"

Ray said no more but followed the steward out into the passage, round the corner and into another cabin. This was about the same size as Mrs. Wiley's but had four beds in it and a chest of drawers. It seemed very crowded.

"You're one of the lucky ones," said the steward. "You've got this all to yourself until we get to Naples, when a couple of Swiss gentlemen come aboard. This is your bed. Number five hundred and seventeen."

Number five hundred and seventeen was an upper berth with a small porthole through which it was possible to see a part of the customs shed. It was strange to think the ship was still tied up to land; Ray had the feeling he'd been aboard a couple of days already.

"What about the other bed?" he asked.

"That'll be empty all the way, I expect. You might get someone at Colombo, though."

"Someone black?" asked Ray.

The steward grinned. "Could be," he said. "Well, I'll be around if you want me. There's a card on the chest that tells you the times of meals, and there's a pamphlet with lots of information about the ship. Do you like sugar in your tea?"

"Yes, please," said Ray.

"I might bring you a cup first thing. Children under twelve aren't supposed to get morning tea, but I might stretch a point for you seeing as you're all by yourself in here."

The steward went and Ray began to examine the cabin. It wasn't like a bedroom at all, but more like some corner of a factory with pipes and tubes and iron girders in a complicated tangle all over the ceiling. In the middle there were four round metal things about the size of grapefruit, with holes in them through which air was blowing. Ray experimented and found that they could be turned in their sockets so as to blow air in any direction around the cabin. They could also be set in one position which turned the air off.

All the drawers in the chest were empty, so Ray dragged his small suitcase from under the bed and began to arrange his clothes in the top drawer. His small traveling clock in a leather case, which his teacher had given him, he opened up and put on the

shelf over his bed. The room still lacked something, so he opened the drawer again and took out a
large round yellow pebble which he had brought
back from a holiday in Cornwall one year, and the
red felt pennant with the picture of an eagle on it
which he had got free with an issue of a comic paper.
He draped the pennant so that it hung from the shelf,
and put the pebble on top to keep it in place. Now it
looked more like home. Ray climbed up into his
berth and lay with his hands behind his head and his
eyes closed, feeling for a moment neither happy nor
unhappy. The blowers made a roaring sound, at first
annoying and then soothing. He felt himself drifting
off, pulled himself awake again, drifted and finally
slept.

He awakened suddenly, and almost with a feeling of panic, to find himself the center of a most tremendous din. Gradually he sorted the noises out—the roar of the blowers, some children shouting in the passage outside, and finally a mechanical pounding that shook the whole cabin. It must be the ship's engines. Ray pressed his face close to the thick glass of the porthole.

It was quite dark outside but he could see a row of lights that could have been on the dock, and as he stared he saw that they were moving. With a shout he jumped off his berth, forgetting the distance he was from the floor, and fell with a thump on the mat. No time to consider bruises, however, and he scrambled to his feet and ran out into the passage. This was blocked by half a dozen children of various ages, all with very fair hair, who must have come aboard since Ray fell asleep, for he had not seen them before.

"We're moving," he cried to them. "Don't you want to see us go?"

They all stared at him with blank expressions but did not move, so Ray pushed past them and ran up the stairs. He went up five decks with two flights of stairs to each deck and fourteen stairs to each flight, which made one hundred and forty stairs, and emerged into the open air panting and feeling slightly dizzy. There were twenty or thirty people standing against the rail, but still plenty of room for him.

The dock was already ten or twelve yards away and the gap was widening. In between lay the gray-green water, swirling up mud and oil as the ship's engines went astern, and a strong smell of wetness and decay began to rise. Two tugs were pulling the *Huron's* stern around, black, acrid smoke belching from their funnels. A sailor standing right against the stern rail of the *Huron* kept blowing sharp blasts on a whistle and being answered from the tugs' hooters.

Only a couple of dozen people stood on the wet dockside and waved. One twisted colored paper streamer still joined someone on the ship to someone on shore; then it snapped and one high-pitched voice cheered. Ray felt that no one seemed to care very much whether the ship sailed or stayed. Some men were pushing the gangway back alongside the shed, and when they had it in place they turned and walked away without a single look at the *Huron*.

A man standing by Ray said, "You get the worst sendoff in the world from Tilbury. You want to see how they do it in Melbourne or Hobart. Londoners are a lot of wet cabbage leaves."

Ray didn't care for this, but it really hadn't been

much of a sendoff and there didn't seem to be anything he could say. So he changed the subject by saying, "I'm going to Hobart."

"Good on yer," said the man. "It's a lovely city. You'll like it and that's for sure."

Ray felt more determined than ever that he would not, but had enough sense to keep the feeling to himself. He stared at the lights getting smaller and then at the smoky haze over London glowing with an orange light from the street lights and the neon signs, and wondered if he would ever see it again. He had never thought of England as being the place where he belonged; he had thought of towns or streets or houses as being home, but now suddenly it was a whole country. And it was disappearing in a mess of smoke and darkness for the last time, and no one

seemed to care. He could not watch it any longer but with a shiver turned away from the rail and went below into the warmth and light and bustle.

On his own deck the children were still playing and he suddenly realized why they had not taken any notice of him before. They were all foreign children, speaking to each other in words that did not sound like a sensible language at all but just a jumble of sounds. One of the boys, a short, sturdy chap of about his own age, was standing right in front of the door of Ray's cabin. He had fair, almost yellow, hair like the others and wore a round woven cap on the back of his head. When he saw Ray coming he moved aside and smiled slightly. Ray tried to smile back but somehow his face felt stiff and unmovable; he stood in the doorway and the two boys looked at each other for what seemed to be a long time.

"Anti! Anti! Tule mukaan!"

The boy looked down the passage to where a woman was leaning out of a doorway and beckoning to him, and answered something in his own language. Then he turned to Ray again and pointing his finger toward himself he said, "Anti!"

Ray guessed this must be the boy's name, so he repeated it. The boy nodded, pleased. Then he pointed at Ray.

"Ray," said Ray.

"Ray?" said the other boy, and when Ray nodded his face suddenly broke into a wide smile. And the first thing Ray noticed was that two of Anti's top teeth were missing. So then he grinned broadly too and showed his own bare gums, and in a moment they were both grinning and laughing and pointing at each other as if it were the funniest thing in the world that both of them should have gaps where their top front teeth ought to have been.

3. Tea before bed

Ray went up on deck once more before turning in for the night, but there was very little to see. A thick mist lay over the river and although he knew they must be passing places he was familiar with, like Herne Bay, Margate and Broadstairs, he could see nothing of them. The ship seemed to be following a line of buoys that had red flashing lights on them. Some of them had bells that tolled rather sadly as the buoy rocked. As the buoys appeared ahead he could hear the bell striking slowly in time with the waves. Then as the ship drew level and the buoy began to tip in the bow wave the bell sounded more urgent, and finally, as the ship passed and the churned-up water from the screws made the buoy dance wildly, the bell beat out madly as if for a fire.

Down below in the cabin Mrs. Wiley was preparing a little supper party. She had brought a teapot, tea and a can of condensed milk, and she was just taking a box of cookies out of her case when Ray poked his head around the door to say good night.

"Just in time," she said. "Take this teapot and ask the first steward you see where the boiling water is."

"How do you know there is some?" Ray asked.

"There always is. I'm an old hand at this trip," said Mrs. Wiley. "There'll be a tap somewhere. Be careful, don't scald yourself."

Ray trudged off grumbling to himself. Mind how you go—look both ways before you cross the road— hold it tight in case you drop it—don't scald yourself —older people seemed to think boys were just natur- ally not sensible. As if he'd never filled a pot of tea before!

On the landing outside the cabins he came on a steward he had not seen before, a rather disheveled, unshaven one with his jacket unbuttoned at the neck. However, he was obviously a steward, so Ray asked where he could find the boiling water.

The steward answered in a thick Irish accent.

"It's meself that'll have to show yer," said the stew- ard good-naturedly and, beckoning, led the way up to the next deck and into a small room marked SERV- ICE PANTRY. In this there was a sink, a large refrigerator, some aluminum-topped benches and two ladies filling babies' bottles with milk and warm- ing them in hot water. The steward pointed to an odd-shaped tap over one of the benches.

"And don't be after putting the tea leaves in the sinks, for 'tis blocked they'll be and me crawling on my belly like a heathen snake trying to poke them clear."

"All right," said Ray. "Thank you."

"Shall I be giving you a hand? It's an awkward tap if you've not had the using of it before."

"I'll manage," said Ray between his teeth.

"Sure you'll manage," said the steward, quite undisturbed by Ray's rudeness. "And it's meself that's the old granny to be sure."

Ray went over to the tap, put the pot under it and turned the odd-shapped handle. Nothing happened. He tried turning it the other way. A single drop of steaming water dropped into his pot. He was about to ask one of the women how the thing worked but his pride got the better of him. He fiddled with the top of the tap again and more or less by accident pressed down on it. Immediately a jet of steam and a spluttering of water shot out, some of it striking the rim of the teapot and splashing the back of his hand. Ray yelled and almost dropped the pot. The steward, who had gone away, came back and looked in through the doorway.

"Isn't it the best thing now for people to find things out for themselves," he said with a grin, and the two ladies laughed.

Ray scowled at the teapot and kept his back to them. He filled the pot with boiling water, holding it well up under the tap now that he knew what to expect. Then he put the lid in place cautiously and carried the pot out, taking care not to look at any of them. As soon as he was on the stairs one of the women said something and the others laughed. Ray only heard the laughter and flushed with embarrassment. There were three blisters on the back of his hand as large as pennies and they were beginning to sting. He felt that if he did not clench his teeth together very hard there would be tears in his eyes soon.

"Ah, here's the tea now," said Mrs. Wiley with satisfaction. "Did you have any trouble getting the water?"

230770

"No," said Ray, and having put the pot down hid his scalded hand behind his back.

"Sit down on Ila's bed and have a cookie while I pour the tea, then."

"I don't want anything," said Ray.

"Oh, but Ray . . ."

Ray didn't feel he could stay and argue so he went quickly from the cabin and back to his own. There he climbed up on to his bunk and lay face down on the pillow feeling wretched. He let his bad hand hang over the side in the air from the blowers so that it did not hurt quite so much. In this position and with nothing else to occupy his mind he noticed again how the ship's engines shook the whole cabin. The latch of the door rattled; the high wooden side of his bed, put there, he supposed, to prevent his rolling out in his sleep, played a tune against the iron bed; a glass from which he had drunk water earlier jiggled against the side of the goblet; even the steel sheets that made up the wall of the cabin creaked and groaned. And behind it all was the steady whirr of machinery and the thumping of the screws. He thought he would never be able to sleep in such a racket.

In fact he dozed off almost at once and woke again with a start only a few seconds later to the sound of glass breaking. In a dreamy sort of way he thought the glass of the porthole must have broken and that any moment the sea would be pouring in on him. But a glance showed the porthole was still whole. The trouble was inside the cabin where the water goblet had slid across the top of the chest with the movement of the ship and crashed to the ground. There was a dark wet patch on the carpet. Almost immediately the cabin steward put his head in. He looked at the glass and the spilt water and then at Ray.

"Well, you're a fine one, I don't think," he said. "Fancy leaving the goblet on top of the chest. Didn't you notice there's a special rack for it, and the glasses? We're on a ship, now, you know."

This was too much for Ray. "I didn't know it would slip off," he said, and his voice came out wavery instead of straight the way he meant it to. "Nobody told me. Can't you leave me alone!"

The steward stepped over the broken glass and came right up to the bunk with a look of concern on his face. "I say," he said. "You are in a bad way, aren't you? Sorry if I was a bit sharp with you."

Ray didn't answer. He had turned his face to the wall, and now lay perfectly still, breathing heavily.

"You needn't worry about the goblet," the steward went on. "People are always breaking them. I'll get a new one tomorrow."

Ray made an impatient movement of his shoulders but still did not speak.

35

"Oh, well, if that's the way you feel. Pity though, because I was just coming along to ask if you'd do me a favor."

There was a silence, and then very slowly Ray raised his head and turned it to face the steward.

"What favor?" he asked faintly.

"One of these foreign families," said the steward. "They're in trouble. The purser's made a mistake and put a family of five in a four-berth cabin. They're from Finland, you see, and they don't seem to understand a word of English. So they didn't know how to tell anybody that one of them hasn't got a bed. I just went in there and found two of these kids squashed up together like a couple of sardines. Well, I mean, we can't have that, can we?"

Ray lifted his head off the pillow. "What are you going to do?" he said. "Why not use the spare bunk in here? I don't mind."

"I was hoping you'd say that," said the steward. "The purser's office is closed now so I can't fix anything until the morning. But if you wouldn't mind one of these kids spending just the one night here, that would solve it, wouldn't it?"

"All right," said Ray.

"I'll just pick up this glass," said the steward.

Ray waited for a long time, it seemed, and nothing happened. Then, when he was almost ready to drop off to sleep again a figure in bright orange-striped pajamas came shyly through the door, followed almost immediately by the steward with an armful of clothes.

"Well, here we are," said the steward cheerfully. "Here's your lodger. I don't know his name . . ."

"I do," said Ray, propping himself up on his elbow and smiling. "It's Anti."

Anti came sharply to attention in the middle of the room, bowed his head with a quick ducking movement, then grinned and jumping forward grabbed Ray's hand and shook it vigorously. Ray was taken by surprise, and the sudden pain in his scalded hand made him cry out and try to snatch it away. Anti jumped away as if expecting a blow and retreated to the far corner of the cabin.

"Sorry," said Ray. "It's my bad hand. I scalded it."

"Let's have a look," said the steward. "Um, that's not so good. Why didn't you say something before? Here, come here, what's-your-name, Anti. Look! Hurt."

He pointed to the blisters on the back of Ray's hand and then shook his own and put it between his knees making a face as if he were in excruciating agony. Anti stared at the blisters and then, muttering something in Finnish, darted away.

"Now what's he up to?" said the steward. "Have we frightened him or something?"

Anti was back again in a few seconds, however,

with a small tube of ointment. He showed the tube
to Ray, but as the writing was also in Finnish that
didn't help; then he squeezed some of the ointment
on to the back of Ray's hand and very gently with
one fingertip smeared it over the sore places. In ten
seconds the pain had gone.

"It's better!" exclaimed Ray, holding up his hand
and wiggling the fingers. "It's better already!"

"Proper little medicine man, isn't he?" said the
steward.

Anti did not understand a word of this but he
seemed to guess what was meant. He smiled with
pleasure and after screwing the top of the tube on
again he placed it on the chest. He pointed to it and
then at Ray's hand.

The steward said, "I expect he means you're to use
it again if you want to."

"Thank you," said Ray, speaking slowly and clearly. "Thank you very much."

"Sank you muk," said Anti with another bob of his head. Then he climbed agilely to the other top bunk and sat there grinning and showing the empty space between his teeth. Ray grinned back in the same way. It was almost as if it were a secret sign of some sort.

"You're a couple of beauties and no mistake," said the steward. "I can see you'll hit it off all right. See you in the morning."

When he had gone Ray undressed and got into his pajamas, which had faded blue stripes and were not nearly so gay as Anti's. He found a couple of caramels in his pocket and threw one to the Finnish boy. Then he climbed back into his own bunk and they lay sucking and staring at each other across the cabin.

A minute or so later the cabin door opened again, this time for Mrs. Wiley carrying a cup of tea and some cookies. "I thought you might have changed your mind," she said in an anxious voice. "You don't have to drink it if you don't want to."

"Thanks," said Ray. "I think I would like it after all."

"Good," said Mrs. Wiley. She put the cup and the cookies down on the chest and then went out again looking happier. She did not even notice Anti.

When the door had shut the two boys giggled. Then Ray poured half the tea into a glass and gave it and one of the cookies to Anti. "Your share," he said.

Anti took them and bobbed his head, then he frowned and stared hard at the ceiling for quite a long time. Suddenly his face cleared and he said slowly, "Sank . . . a-muk!"

4. I'm a good sailor

Next morning Ray awakened feeling odd—rather as if he had been changed into someone else during the night. He did not know how Anti felt for there was no way of asking. They made a race of washing and dressing and when they were almost ready the steward came with the morning tea. He asked them if they had been able to find the showers.

Ray shivered, thinking of the cold showers after physical training classes at school. "Cold showers on a morning like this?" he asked.

"Hot showers," said the steward. "There are six of them up on the next deck. Nothing like a shower for freshening you up in the morning."

Ray started to take his clothes off again, and Anti, with a look of complete mystification, copied him. The steward went through an act in the middle of the cabin, pretending to be in a shower, soaping himself, rubbing his hair and spluttering, all in a very realistic manner. Anti understood right away and found his soap and towel.

On the way up the stairs and along the passages looking for the showers, the boys discovered that they could not walk in straight lines, but were tilted from side to side of the passage, so that they kept bumping into each other and had to grab the handrail now and then. They made a joke of it.

"It must be pretty rough," Ray said, and then carried away by the idea, added, "I say, I hope it beats up into a real storm with the ship pitching up and down, like you see in the movies sometimes . . ." He did a dipping, switchback movement with his hands.

Anti nodded, and then putting both hands to his middle made a long, agonized face and pretended to heave. Ray hadn't thought of that side of it and laughed uneasily. "I'm not going to be seasick," he announced. "I'm a good sailor."

The door right where they were standing opened and out came Andrew Newman, rubbing his thin dark hair on the corner of his towel and looking even more like a seal. "Looking for the shower, are you?" he said. "Well, take my advice; don't use number two or number five. They haven't been adjusted properly and run cold all the time."

"You know everything, don't you?" said Ray a little sharply.

Andrew grinned. "I'm just naturally curious," he said. "I tried them all." He turned his attention to Anti and after looking him up and down carefully said to Ray, "Who you got here, then? Looks like one of those queer foreigners." He prodded Anti with one finger. "Say something foreign!" he commanded.

Anti looked surprised and turned to Ray.

"Gabble-gabble-gabble," said Andrew. "Go on! Ipsi wopsi popsi quee!"

"Leave him alone, can't you?" said Ray angrily.

Andrew laughed loudly. Then he flicked Anti's ankle with the corner of his wet towel and went off down the passage singing "Ipsi wopsi popsi quee," to a madeup tune. Ray clenched his fists and found that he was already beginning to hate Andrew Newman. And by contrast he was drawn closer to the Finnish boy. As there was no way of putting this into words, he made a gargoyle's face after the retreating Andrew, and then winked at Anti, who immediately laughed delightedly.

They had their showers, dressed again and went up on C deck to look at the weather. The deck was almost empty. A cold wind was blowing across it, the wood was slimy with wetness and heavy drips fell from the keels of the lifeboats. A man and his wife, both thin and bony, in long raincoats, walked up and down, up and down one side of the deck, stamp-

43

ing their feet as they turned. Ray heard the man say, "It's just over forty yards. If we do twenty a morning we shall have walked half a mile."

"That ought to be enough," said his wife.

Ray thought she did not look as if she would last that far.

On another part of the deck a short man in white trousers and white shirt was skipping vigorously. He nodded and smiled at them but did not speak because he was counting.

"This is pretty mad," Ray said. He and Anti went over to the rail and stood there a little while watching the sea. It was a sad grayish-green color but it did not seem very rough. Nevertheless, the ship was

rolling steadily from side to side, although as they were standing on it they had the feeling that it was the sea that was moving, washing up the sky on one side and then the other like the water in the bath when you roll over suddenly.

Ray found he was staring at the dark line that separated sea and sky as if hypnotized. Up and down it went, up and down, up and . . . up . . . The rail he was holding seemed about to be plunged into the water and he with it, then slowly the rolling movement came to an end, the ship hung for what seemed a long time in doubt and then began the long movement back again.

"Whew!" said Ray. "I thought she was going to roll right over that time."

He turned away from the rail in time to see the bony man leading his wife toward the staircase. Her face was quite gray. "It didn't take much to upset her," Ray said with a laugh. "I expect it will get much worse yet. They say the Bay of Biscay is always pretty dreadful."

He caught sight of the clock just then and saw it was only a few minutes to eight. Breakfast time. He made signals to Anti to indicate eating and said, "Breakfast!"

"Brekfuss," Anti agreed and went with him to the stairs.

45

In the dining room, which was on F deck, the chief waiter stood just inside the door. He was a short, sour-looking man with thinning gray hair. "What are you boys up to?" he asked suspiciously. Obviously he was one of those people who take it for granted that boys are always up to something.

"We want some breakfast," said Ray.

"Brekfuss," echoed Anti.

The chief waiter asked their berth numbers and then looked at a long list. "Tables six and seven," he said, pointing. "Over there!"

The boys went over and sat down self-consciously at one of the tables. Only two people had arrived at it so far—two bronzed young men with curly hair, open-necked shirts and a look about them as if they were used to hard work. They were eating cereal and talking to each other in a language that sounded like English but wasn't. Ray guessed it was Dutch. When the waiter came he turned out to be a Scot, and Ray was beginning to wonder if he and the bedroom steward were the only Englishmen on the boat.

Ray ordered orange juice. Anti shrugged his shoulders at the menu, not being able to understand it. "Better bring the same for both of us," said Ray.

After the orange juice they had scrambled eggs, and then, as there seemed to be so many things on the menu that it seemed a pity to waste them, Ray ordered sausages, liver and tomatoes. While he was waiting for this to come he wondered what had happened to Mrs. Wiley and Ila. Perhaps he ought to have awakened them or said where he was.

He looked around and noticed how few people there were in the dining room. He also noticed that the ship was rolling quite a lot again; an empty glass slid across the table toward him and he just caught it before it fell off the edge of the table. A moment later there was a tremendous crash from the other side of the dining room; a pile of plates had skidded off a side table and hit the floor.

"That's a good start," said the waiter who had just arrived with racks of toast for the Dutchmen and two plates loaded with sausages, liver and tomatoes for Ray and Anti. "They were clean plates, too," he said. "Wouldn't have been so bad if they'd been dirty ones."

"I suppose a lot get broken during the voyage," said Ray, staring at his plate and suddenly realizing that he could not possibly eat another mouthful.

"Och, that's nothing," said the waiter. "Just you wait till lunch time and we're well into the Bay. It'll be like a madhouse, I tell you. She's a shocking boat, the *Huron*. No stabilizers, you see. Just rolls about like an old log. There goes another pile!"

47

There was another crash of breaking plates; Ray was both excited and shocked, thinking of how much fuss his mother used to make over one broken cup. The thought, however, made him sad and when he looked at his food again it looked even more uneatable. But you couldn't order food and then just leave it. Anti was already attacking his as if he'd not eaten for a week. Ray slowly picked up his knife and fork and dug the prongs into one of the sausages. Grease welled out of the skin where he had prodded it. He changed his mind and put a very small piece of tomato in his mouth. He had to make quite an effort to swallow it.

He put his knife and fork down again and took a mouthful of coffee. Then he tried again, this time actually cutting a sausage and getting the piece as far as his lips. But the hot, greasy smell of it was too much for him. His throat felt as if it were closing right up; his eyes felt strained and too big for their sockets. He quickly dropped his knife and fork and made a dash for the door.

Outside in the lounge people were sitting waiting for the second sitting of breakfast. Ray did not notice them; he was staring wildly around, wondering if he could possibly get right down to his cabin before being sick. However, a steward pushing an electric floor polisher up and down the lounge glanced up and seemed to know immediately what the trouble was.

"First door on the right with a red light over it," he said. "I shouldn't hang about if I were you."

Ray did not hang about; he ran, just reaching the door with the red light in time.

A few minutes later Ray emerged into the passage again, feeling weak and hollow and with no interest in the ship at all except to find his way as quickly as possible to his berth. The ship seemed to be rolling and tipping more than ever so that he could not understand how other people were making their way about so easily. He clung to the rail all along the passage and all the way down the stairs, taking no notice of the sympathetic faces or sympathetic noises he encountered on the way. At the foot of the stairs he almost ran into Ila. She was just standing looking up the stairs with a glazed look in her eyes.

"I thought I'd go up to breakfast," she said, but without conviction.

"Sausages," said Ray.

Ila gulped. "My favorite," she said in a dull voice, and then, "Oh dear!" And she turned and almost ran back to her cabin.

Ray couldn't help feeling a sly satisfaction at this, but the feeling did not last long. He, too, soon staggered across the landing and into his own cabin. He

did not even have the strength to climb up on to his own bed but tumbled head first on to one of the lower bunks and lay flat and still.

For the rest of the morning Ray lay there. As long as he kept his head on the same level as his body the ship did not seem to be moving so much, but the instant he raised his head the feeling came over him again. The bedroom steward came in and made up the beds. He put a sort of tin bucket— really for rubbish and called by the stewards a "Rosie"—near the head of Ray's bed.

"It'll pass," he said, but was too busy clearing up to waste time on sympathy.

Anti came down to the cabin two or three times, and patted Ray's shoulder and smiled at him, and even drew up a stool and sat by him for ten minutes or so. But there was nothing they could talk about. In the end he took a Finnish comic book from his suitcase and gave it to Ray, then went off again.

I'm a Good Sailor

Just before lunch time the bedroom steward came in and said, "You ought to try and eat something, you know. You'll get over it quicker if you eat."

"I don't want anything," said Ray miserably.

"No, I know you don't. But you ought to force yourself. It's no good lying there and feeling sorry for yourself. I've just been saying the same thing to your mum and your sister."

"Mrs. Wiley isn't my mother," said Ray. "Is she feeling sick, too?"

"She's much worse than you are," said the steward. "And you're not sick. You've just given up without trying, that's all. Sick? You don't know the meaning of the word. I was just like you on my first trip. Lying about groaning and feeling sorry for myself and all the rest of it. But the other chaps wouldn't let me. They made me get up and polish brasses."

Ray groaned. "That was cruel," he said.

"Cruel? Not a bit of it. I had a Rosie in one hand in case I needed it, and a polishing cloth in the other. And I did a bit of polishing and felt dreadful, and did some more, and felt worse, and then I thought, well, the job's got to be done and I stopped feeling sick and got on with it. And believe it or not, I've never been seasick since that day. Touch wood!" He looked around for some wood to touch, for there isn't much on a ship, and eventually patted his own head.

Ray swung his feet off the bunk and sat up rather groggily. "Have you got any brass you want polished?" he asked.

"That's the style," said the steward. "We'll make a sailor of you yet. You can make a start on the door handles. Come on! And bring the Rosie with you!"

5. Airmail from Hobart

There were four bedroom stewards on H deck, Frank,
Tich, Wally and Studs, and during that day they
all managed to find little jobs to keep Ray busy. He
polished door handles, counted towels, filled water
goblets and then as a special treat was allowed to use
the electric floor polisher which was a machine sort
of like a lawn mower with a large whirling brush
instead of cutting blades. He was also allowed to
call the stewards by their Christian names. The
steward who looked after his cabin was Frank.

Ray missed his lunch, but by the middle of the
afternoon he was feeling much better. He had a sort
of dull headache and a tired feeling in his back, but
by four o'clock he discovered he had something of an
appetite. He had just finished tidying the cups and
saucers in Frank's cupboard when the first suspicion
of hunger came over him.

"Do you mind if I leave this and go and get some
tea?" he said.

Frank laughed. "That's what I like to hear," he said. "Shows you're feeling better. And while you're up there, ask one of the waiters if you can bring two cups of tea down here to the cabin."

"For you?" asked Ray.

"No, I just thought your mother and sister might be feeling like a cup."

"Mrs. Wiley's not my mother," said Ray.

"No, that's right," said Frank. "But all the same I expect she likes a cup of tea now and then."

Ray realized that he had not been into Mrs. Wiley's cabin all day to see how she was, and felt a little ashamed. "I'll do that," he said.

There was tea at each of the tables in the dining room, and large trays of cakes were arranged on the side tables so that people could choose their own. At home it had always been one cake each at tea time, or two on special occasions. Ray was standing in front of the trays wondering whether to count this as a special occasion, when a bigger boy pushed past him with a plate heaped high with at least half a dozen cakes. Ray licked his lips and looked carefully over the trays to make his choice. A doughnut first because that was his favorite, then a slice of battenburg with marzipan round the edge, an apricot jam tart, a slice of fruit cake for filling up corners . . . he hesitated in front of a heap of chocolate cream éclairs. Better not perhaps; not today in any case. Maybe tomorrow he would have two to make up for it. He took his plate to the table.

The waiters had damped the tablecloth and put wooden ledges round the table to prevent the plates from sliding off when the ship rolled. Ray hadn't thought about what the ship was doing for hours, but now he saw, from the way the tea in his cup kept swinging about, that, in fact, it was rolling as much as ever. The only difference was he did not mind it. From his place at the table he could see the water through a porthole rising and falling so as to make the view first all sky and then all sea. Instead of depressing him it made him feel quite excited. After all, it was silly to be at sea if you did not feel it. However, he did not wish for a storm this time.

Before he had finished Anti came and sat down next to him. With him were two adults and a small girl, and it was easy to see that they all belonged to the same family. Anti jogged Ray's arm and pointed first to the girl. "Serpa!" he said.

Ray guessed this was her name. He hadn't much time for small girls, but he smiled at her and said hello. Serpa was so embarrassed that she put her face right down out of sight so that her forehead almost touched the edge of the table and all that could be seen of her were two pigtails of fair hair with red bows. Anti's father was not so shy, however. He was a short, bony-faced man with mild blue eyes. His hands were very large and powerful looking and in one of them he carried a tiny dictionary about the size of a matchbox. He smiled at Ray and then after flicking through the dictionary for a while said, "You good friend to Anti?"

"Yes," said Ray. "We've been having fun."

"Fun?" said the man and turned to his dictionary. After a long pause he said, "You go Australia?" And when Ray nodded he went on, "Is good in Australia. Plenty work, plenty sunshine."

Ray was just going to say that he didn't want to go to Australia himself when it struck him that this might be difficult to understand. Instead he heard himself saying, "Yes, Australia very nice."

They all grinned delightedly at each other. Ray thought how terrible it would be for them if they did not like it in Australia. Even worse for them than for him.

When he had finished his tea he took two cups down to Mrs. Wiley and Ila; they were still lying on their beds, Mrs. Wiley reading and Ila staring miserably at the wall of the cabin.

"Well, that was nice of you, Ray," said Mrs. Wiley. "I was thinking of getting up, but Ila felt so bad I stayed with her. Haven't you been sick at all?"

"I was a bit queer this morning," said Ray. "But it passed off." He did not feel like telling the whole story. "There were wonderful cakes for tea. Cream buns and chocolate éclairs and everything."

Ila groaned. "Shut up, you little beast," she said.

To prevent an argument Mrs. Wiley said quickly, "Oh, while I remember, Ray—there's a letter from your Aunt Netta in the top drawer. There's a message for you at the end. It must have come to Tilbury, but it wasn't picked up until yesterday . . . look in the drawer and you'll see it."

Ray opened the drawer and saw the blue airmail letter lying on top and a dreadful feeling came over him; he thought of what it would be like going to strangers in a strange land, where it would be summer at Christmas time, and where he didn't have a single friend. He suddenly felt how alone he was in the world, small and helpless, pushed from here to there regardless of how he felt. He shivered as if he had felt a draft, and closed the drawer again.

"What's the matter? Didn't you find it?" said Mrs. Wiley. "I'm sure I put it there."

"It's there all right," said Ray. "I just don't feel like reading it, that's all."

"But there was a bit specially for you," said Mrs. Wiley. "And she said such nice things about looking forward to seeing you. And about how she's got a photo of you when you were eight that your mother sent her . . ."

"I don't want to read it!" cried Ray and ran violently out of the cabin.

"Well!" exclaimed Mrs. Wiley as the door slammed. "I don't know what to make of him, and that's a fact."

Ila rolled over on her bed and groaned. "I do feel awful," she said.

"What do you expect me to do?" cried her mother in an exasperated voice. "Hold the ship still for you or something? I don't know which of you is the worst, and that's a fact; Ray and his miseries, or you pretending to be sick!"

"I'm not pretending!" howled Ila.

"Not much!" said Mrs. Wiley, and returned to her book.

When Ray ran out of the cabin he went around the corner with his head down and crashed straight into Frank and sent him flying. They sat up and looked at each other, Ray rubbing the top of his head, Frank holding his middle. Then they both burst out laughing.

"Well, what was all that about?" asked Frank when they were both on their feet again. "Who were you running away from? The ghost of H deck?"

"I didn't know there was a ghost," said Ray.

"There isn't," said Frank. "Unless he's the one who's hidden my best polishing cloth."

"Oh, that was me," said Ray. "I've got it in my drawer for safety."

"Hand over!" Frank demanded.

When they were in Ray's cabin Frank said more seriously, "Come on, tell uncle. What's the trouble? You were in a bit of a state just now, weren't you?"

"Well, I suppose I was," Ray admitted.

"I thought that was a sort of tear in your eye, too."

59

"It might have been," said Ray, rubbing his eyes on his shirt sleeve. "Well . . ."

"Yes?"

After a moment's hesitation Ray tried to tell Frank how he felt about going to Hobart to this aunt he had never seen before. "I suppose it's kind of her to ask me," he said. "But I don't want people to be kind, I just want them to be ordinary. I hate people being kind to me, or sorry for me."

"I must remember that and give you a good beating every now and then," Frank said.

"No, I didn't really mean that. I meant I hate being the sort of person that people have to be sorry for—like a cripple or someone with a dreadful disease. That's what it feels like being me . . . as if I had some disease . . ."

"Um," said Frank. "I think I see what you mean. I must have a think about that . . . and meanwhile, how would you like to have a look around the ship? In the crew's quarters and the engineroom and the places where little boys aren't supposed to go!"

Ray cheered up immediately. "I say," he said. "Can you take me?"

"Special favor," said Frank. "Me and the captain are old school chums."

Ray smiled.

"Don't you believe me?"

"No," said Ray.

60

"Good for you; we really weren't. Come on!"

They went up on to G deck and along the passage, past the showers and the special tap for ice water, past the baggage room and then on still farther into a strange part of the ship. This was the crew's quarters, and although it did not look any different, Ray felt that in some way it was different.

"Mess room," said Frank.

This was a large place with long tables. The tables were in a mess all right. There were dirty plates and dishes, spilled tea, crusts, butter dishes with only a smear of butter left—all the clutter of meals not cleared away. Half a dozen members of the crew were eating or smoking and talking at the tables and they barely glanced up at Ray. The bearded deckhand, Arthur Dobbs, was there and grinned before turning his attention back to a plate of sausages and chips.

"Do you call it a mess room because it's in such a mess?" Ray asked. A wet tea cloth sailed across the room and caught him under the ear.

"What was that for?" he demanded indignantly.

"Cracking old jokes," Frank said. "You're lucky it wasn't a boot that hit you."

"It wasn't meant to be a joke at all," said Ray, rubbing his ear.

Frank showed him the cabin where he and five other members of the crew spent their time off duty and slept when they got the chance. It was big compared with the cabins on H deck, but as there was a record player going at one end, a harmonica at the other, and a fellow mending his own shoes in between, it did not seem anywhere nearly big enough for all the noise it contained.

"Imagine trying to sleep in all this," Frank bawled. "And some of these characters are capable of keeping it up till one in the morning."

The sailor mending his own shoes suspended his hammer in the air for a moment and said, "Trouble with you bedroom stewards is you don't have enough work to keep you busy. If you were down in the engineroom with us you'd get too tired to worry about a little bit of noise. I never have any trouble sleeping."

62

"You never really wake up," retorted Frank.

"Slob!" said the man from the engineroom and gave his shoe a vicious wallop.

Frank looked at his watch and said, "I can't show you any more today because I'm due back on duty soon. Another time, perhaps, you'd like to see the engines."

"Yes, please," said Ray.

"I'll see how things go," said Frank. "Now we'd better go back."

On the way he started to talk about Hobart, telling Ray what a fine place it was, with more sunshine than you ever got in England, fine sandy beaches only a mile or so from the center of the city, and the great mountain just behind where you could go picnicking on Sunday. "Some friends of mine took me up there last time I was in Hobart," he said. "We lit a fire of stringy bark and grilled chops in the open air. That was really something."

Ray did not answer; in fact he was hardly listening. He had just remembered that he never had the puppy that was to be a birthday present. "If I'd stayed in England I should have had a puppy by now," he said.

"I expect your aunt will let you have one in Hobart," Frank said.

"That's not the same thing at all," said Ray sadly.

6. Cold for a swim

The swimming pool on C deck was filled with sea water as soon as the *Huron* was clear of the Thames, but of course no one actually swam in it. The weather was far too cold—gray and overcast with a hard cold wind that made you wish for blazing fires or warm overcoats. Once the *Huron* had passed Gibraltar and entered the Mediterranean the skies cleared and there was good sunshine from the hard blue sky. It was still not swimming weather though, because the water in the pools was drawn up from the deep cold sea they sailed through first.

The day after passing Gibraltar Ray and Anti were sitting in the lounge playing checkers. At the next table was another group of boys, among whom was Andrew Newman. They were making a lot of noise and throwing checkers at one another. By and by one of the stewards came across to stop them.

"You ought to be able to find something more sensible to do than that," he said. "Why don't you go up on deck where you won't be annoying other people?"

"There's nothing to do on deck," said one of the boys. "There's nothing to do interesting on the whole ship. People just sitting around . . ."

"You could go for a swim," said the steward. "Might cool some of you off a bit."

The boys jeered and laughed at this, but Andrew jumped to his feet, unable to resist the temptation to draw attention to himself. "You think we daren't," he said loudly.

The steward shrugged his shoulders. Most people on the ship were by now a little tired of Andrew.

"That's right," he said. "You daren't."

"Soon show you!" exclaimed Andrew loudly and bustled off to get his swimming trunks.

The steward grinned at the other people in the lounge. "One way of getting rid of him," he said. "Too big for his boots, he is."

"This should be good," said Ray. "Let's go and watch."

"Go and watch?" said Anti, not understanding.

Suddenly Ray felt annoyed. It was always the same; nothing could be said without making a lot of stupid signs and waving his hands about. It was pretty silly when you came to think of it that the only boy on board he was at all friendly with was the one he couldn't talk to. "Oh ... gobble, gobble," he said crossly and, pushing his chair back, he walked away.

As he went up to the open deck he began to feel a little guilty about his behavior. After all, it was far worse for Anti because he couldn't understand anybody. And it would be worse still when he got to Australia and had to go to a school where they spoke English all the time. Still, he didn't have to go! After all, he had a father and a mother. Why didn't they stay at home in Finland? Andrew was right; foreigners were queer.

By the time he had reached the open deck he was beginning to feel that he had misjudged Andrew, who was probably quite nice really. He almost wished he hadn't made friends with Anti—it was always such a bother trying to tell him anything.

About a dozen boys and three or four adults were standing around the swimming pool when Ray got there. Andrew was in his swimming trunks, standing on the edge looking down at the water which was quite clear and faintly blue and looked extremely cold.

"Changed your mind?" shouted one of the spectators.

"Of course not," said Andrew. "I'll be in there in a minute."

"Waiting for a big enough crowd," murmured one of the adults.

Andrew suddenly seemed to make up his mind. "Here goes!" he shouted. "One . . . two . . . three . . .!"

And with that he leaped up in the air and curling his legs up under him, came down with a tremendous splash in the center of the pool. Water shot out in all directions and wet those who were standing fairly close. In the water Andrew squeezed the water out of his hair, screwed his fists into his eyes and bawled out, "It's warm! Come on in!" Nobody made a move to do so.

Just then Anti came to the pool and, seeing no one on the edge, came through the barrier and went right to the edge to look down at the water. "Gobble gobble!" shouted Andrew, his mouth half under the water so that it really did sound something like a turkey. Ray could not help smiling.

A few minutes in the water was long enough. Andrew made for the steps and climbed out and already his teeth were chattering and his legs had become a bluish color. "Here, you ought to have come in," he said to Anti, who was still standing near the edge. "Not so cold as where you come from." He made a rush as he said this and pushed Anti so that he skidded on the side and went with a sharp cry and a splash into the pool. Some of the

boys laughed, but Ray, without stopping to think, jumped the barrier and ran at Andrew. "That was a filthy trick!" he said and grabbed at Andrew's wet arms.

For a moment they wrestled furiously on the side of the pool, not really trying to do anything but simply overcome by anger. Then Ray trod on Andrew's bare toe, and Andrew gave a roar of pain and rage and butted Ray with his head. They rocked on the very edge, trying to keep their balance but refusing to let go of each other. There was a roar from the spectators and then with a mighty splash they both went in.

They crawled up the steps, cold and shivering and feeling on the whole rather miserable, to find the master-at-arms waiting for them with his hands on his hips.

"I saw all of that," he said sternly, "and a very silly exhibition it was."

Andrew started trying to argue, but the master-at-arms cut in with, "I'm in charge here, but if you want to make a fuss about it we'll take it to the captain."

Andrew kept quiet then. The master-at-arms went on to tell them why it was dangerous to push people into the pool, and said that if he caught them at it again he would ban them from using the pool for the rest of the trip. And he finished with, "And if you want to find out who's the best man among you then I suggest you wait until we have the swimming sports in the Indian Ocean, when you can compete against one another in a sportsmanlike way. Now below with you, and get a hot shower and a change of clothing!"

Chastened, the boys went below and did as they were told. Ray said, "You heard what he said? We'll go in for everything in the swimming sports and beat that stuckup Andrew Newman into a cocked hat."

Anti did not understand a word of this but Ray found that he didn't mind; the incident in the pool had drawn them closer together.

7. Naples

Mrs. Wiley could not understand Ray. He seemed quite happy now on the ship going everywhere with that little Finnish boy, jabbering away in bits of English and bits of Finnish and lots of sign language. It was amazing how children managed to get along even when they didn't speak the same language. Yet although he was happy in this way he was still not happy about going to Hobart. Two or three times Mrs. Wiley had tried to persuade Ray to write to his aunt, but Ray just shook his head and gritted his teeth as if she were trying to give him some nasty medicine.

The day before they reached Naples she said to him, "Ila and I are going on one of these coach tours. All around Naples and then out to the volcano and Pompeii—you know, the place that was buried in ashes hundreds and hundreds of years ago. Will you come with us?"

Ray shook his head without even considering it.

"I'd rather stay on board," he said. "I like it on the ship. I wish the voyage could go on forever. I don't like it when we get somewhere. It reminds me about Australia."

"But Hobart's lovely," said Mrs. Wiley. "And anyway, this is Naples. You'll be ever so cross afterward if you refuse a chance to see a great foreign city."

But Ray would have nothing to do with it; he just didn't care.

The following morning when he awakened he felt there was something wrong before he realized that it was simply that the engines had stopped.

Must be Naples, he thought, but instead of rushing up on deck to have a look around he set about doing his usual morning job, which was to help Frank set out the cups for the morning tea. In fact it was not until after breakfast that he went up on deck, and that was only because Anti persuaded him to do so.

The ship was tied up to the dock and a bright, shining metal gangway joined the ship to the shore. There were men in dull gray and blue uniforms with peaked caps at the end of the gangway, and these were no doubt Italian police. Everything was quiet and no one much seemed to be working on the docks near the ship. It was very different from Tilbury, partly because it was so new and clean and partly because of the bright sunshine and the blue sky without a sign of a cloud. The town stretched out before him, rising up the side of a steep slope, and it didn't look at all dirty or smelly. In fact it looked rather lovely. But all the same he didn't want to go and see it.

As he was turning away from the rail Anti jumped on him, dressed in his best clothes and looking very excited. He pointed to himself and then to Naples, and then walked two fingers down the rail. Ray guessed he meant he was going ashore.

Then Anti pointed at Ray as if asking if he were going, so Ray shook his head. "I don't want to," he said.

"Want to?" echoed Anti, putting on a sad expression.

As the passengers went ashore their cabins were locked up and gradually the ship became quieter and quieter, and the only people to be seen were the very old, or parents of very young babies.

Ray stood on deck by the gangway for a while and watched the people going off. The first lot to go were the party who were visiting Vesuvius and Pompeii.

Mrs. Wiley saw Ray and went up to him with her usual worried look. "Are you sure you'll be all right?" she said. "I don't like the idea of leaving you here alone, but Ila hasn't seen Pompeii and I don't want to miss the chance."

"I'll be all right," said Ray.

"Of course you will . . . but all the same . . . are you sure you don't want to change your mind? I expect we could squeeze you in; you could sit on my knee or something . . ."

"Honestly I'd rather not come," said Ray.

"Oh come on, Mum," said Ila in a discontented voice. "We'll miss the coach if you don't hurry."

Mrs. Wiley gave Ray a pat on the arm. "Well, we must go now," she said. "Don't get into any mischief."

As they went down the gangway Ray heard Ila saying, "Fancy saying that to him! He hasn't got the gump to get into mischief. He'll just sit about and mope all day. I think he's a proper little crumb."

Ray blushed furiously and walked away from the rail. He went down to H deck, but Frank seemed to have disappeared, and for a while he wandered around the ship not knowing what to do. In the end he took a book up on C deck and sat in a deck-chair in the warm sunshine and there fell asleep until lunchtime.

When he got down to the dining room he was surprised to find Anti at his table already. "I thought you were going ashore," he said.

Anti looked blank because he had not understood and then went on with his lunch. He seemed depressed and not his usual gay self. Ray wondered what had gone wrong, but knew it was no use asking Anti. As it happened, however, he found out before the end of the meal, for the Finnish translator, a thickset, leathery-faced man with an accent that was half Finnish and half Australian, came over to the table and started to talk to Anti. An energetic conversation went on for some time and then as the translator was leaving Ray summoned up courage to say,

"I thought Anti was going ashore. Anything wrong?"

The translator hesitated. "Well, wrong in a way," he said slowly. "He was going ashore with his family but Mrs. Pyrheinen took sick at the last moment so they couldn't go."

"Mrs. Pyrheinen?"

"That's Anti's mother. It's nothing serious. But they'd paid for the coach tour and it's been a bit of trouble getting the money back. And of course the boy's very disappointed."

Ray smiled at Anti to show that he sympathized, and Anti raised his eyebrows in a comical expression.

During the afternoon both boys found themselves wandering back to the end of the gangway and there standing with their eyes fixed on the distant town. Some of the passengers were already returning to the ship, although in fact it was not due to sail until six o'clock. They were loaded with all sorts of intriguing paper parcels and large cardboard boxes. Ray watched some of the parcels being opened in the lounge, but the things that had been bought were not very interesting to him. A lot of people had bought large walking-talking dolls, or brightly colored coffee tables, as well as musical boxes that played "Come back to Sorrento" when the lids were lifted. One boy had a model car which could be controlled by a little box at the end of a wire. According to which button you pressed the car would turn left or right, stop, go, reverse or flash its headlights. It was quite good really and Ray would have liked to play with it for a while, but of course the boy wouldn't let him. And anyway the battery ran down after a quarter of an hour.

By about half-past three both Anti and Ray were back at the gangway again. Ray had begun to feel that he had been rather silly to stay on board all day. After all, there had been nothing to do; he might just as well have been walking about the town. There was no reason why he shouldn't go now if he wanted to. Even if he only went as far as the first street it would be a change from standing here for hours.

He looked at Anti and wondered how the Finnish lad was feeling; then, making a sudden resolution, he walked boldly on to the gangway and took half a dozen steps along it. Nobody tried to stop him. No one shouted.

He turned back and beckoned to Anti, who only hesitated a second and then scrambled after him. They ran the remaining yards and jumped down onto solid concrete. The two Italian policemen merely smiled at them.

"We're in Italy!" Ray said.

"Italy?" said Anti.

They turned together and made toward the dock gates at a trot.

8. Dates and doughnuts

Naples did not turn out to be at all what Ray had expected. In the first place he had had the idea that when you went to look at a foreign city, the city would just be there, standing about waiting to be looked at. But Naples did not stand about; it seemed to be staring at him for a start, and then running after him and shouting at him.

As soon as he and Anti emerged from the dock gates, the trouble started. Inside, all was quiet and orderly; outside, it was pandemonium. The gates themselves really *were* gates, locked and chained and guarded by policemen. And outside was a collection of ruffianly looking men, dressed in dirty and ragged clothes, and standing pressed up against the bars of the gates so that their arms and even parts of their legs hung through. It was rather like a bit of a movie about the French Revolution. Actually these men were dock workers waiting to be employed, and they had dirty old clothes on because they were going to do dirty work, but Ray did not know this.

The policeman at the gate saw the boys coming and unlocked a little side gate for them, almost pushing them through so that he could lock it again. In front of them was a great wide roadway with four lots of trolley cars and cars apparently going wherever they liked.

"I think the traffic goes on the right in Italy," said Ray.

Then it occurred to him that this wouldn't worry Anti as it probably also went on the right in Finland.

"Buy a nice watch!" said a voice in Ray's ear.

He turned to find a short, smiling man, with a couple of days' growth of beard, but dressed in very stylish and colorful clothing, standing beside him and offering him a very expensive-looking watch. Ray smiled and shook his head and turned back to the important business of crossing the road. He still hadn't sorted out which way the various streams of trolleys and cars were going when Anti made a dash into the middle of it all, and Ray felt he had to dash after him. Horns shrieked, tires made shuddering noises, trolleys rang loud bells, and a large number of drivers yelled. Somehow they both reached the distant curb without being run over. Anti smiled triumphantly.

78

"Very nice watch. Only three pounds," said a voice, and Ray turned to find the same little man at his elbow, looking quite unruffled.

"I don't want a watch," he said. "And anyway I couldn't afford three pounds."

"Two pounds ten shillings," said the man promptly.

In front of them were fine wide streets with cool trees down each side and expensive shops with windows filled with goods. The boys turned to the right along the biggest street. Apart from the queer words written over shops there wasn't anything very foreign or strange here, except the man trying to sell Ray a watch. And he fell into step with them and walked alongside, saying as he did so, "How much you pay for nice watch, eh?"

"Nothing," said Ray, almost shouting. It made him embarrassed to have this queer man hanging on. "I don't want a watch! Don't you understand?"

The man seemed to get the point at last for he put the watch away in his pocket and said, "Sorry, sir." Next moment, however, he pulled his hand out of his pocket clutching two or three pairs of sunglasses. "You buy pair glasses maybe?" he said. "Very chip. I make you special price."

Ray grinned. "I certainly wouldn't want chipped glasses," he said.

The man looked hurt and puzzled. "No like chip?" he said as if finding this hard to believe.

Ray shook his head emphatically. The man put the glasses away still looking puzzled, then he brightened up and produced a tattered printed card and held it out. "Me official guide to Naples," he said proudly. "Show you everything for half a crown."

Actually, Ray had even more than this amount in his pocket, but he did not want to waste money being shown something he could see perfectly well for himself. "Look, do me a favor," he said. "Just go away, please."

Anti caught Ray's sleeve and gave it a jerk, and he turned in time to see two more men in gay clothing running across the road toward them. They both carried an assortment of watches strapped all the way up their arms. "Nice watch!" they were shouting. "Swiss watch, very chip!"

Ray and Anti looked desperately around to see if there was any way to escape, but before they could act they were surrounded. The little man with the two-days' beard said something sharply in Italian to the newcomers, and they replied loudly and angrily. The boys guessed that the first man was trying to warn the others off and telling them not to steal his customers. In a moment it had turned into a shout-

ing match, all three waving their arms and apparently calling each other dreadful names. The boys were hemmed in by arms and bodies and angry faces.

When it looked as if it must surely end in a fight, Ray suddenly dropped to his hands and knees on the pavement and crawled away. Anti was not far behind him, and before the men could see what had become of their customers the boys had dived across the road through the traffic, gone down a narrow side street and then into an even narrower alley off that. Here they paused to get their breath and see if there was to be any pursuit.

After a minute or so it was obvious that they had not been seen and they relaxed and started to look around them. The contrast was amazing. In the main street everything had been spick and span, polished and new; here, not twenty yards off the street, was a grubby, brokendown sort of street, cobbled and littered with all sorts of rubbish. The houses were dilapidated and unpainted, some even without real windows or doors. And all along the street, on lines stretched across from balcony to balcony, was wet gray washing hanging up to dry.

"Talk about flag day," said Ray, pointing up.

They wandered along, staring around them curiously. In one doorway some urchins were crowded around a tin bowl in which a few sticks of a broken-up box were blazing. One of the boys, so dirty and ragged that he might have been specially dressed for a fancy-dress competition, was holding a strip of raw meat over the flames. A woman came out of the darkness of the doorway and handed one of the lads a hunk of dry bread which was immediately shared around. Ray found it hard to understand how you could have expensive American cars running down one street, and in the next this sort of thing.

They went on and after a while the alley ran into a slightly wider cobbled street which climbed steeply up a hill. Here there were one or two shops, or at least openings in the fronts of several houses with goods for sale on trays or rough tables. At one of them there was a little fruit and a jar of immense doughnuts. Ray began to feel quite hungry. He pointed at the doughnuts. "Shall we try one?" he asked Anti. And Anti rubbed his middle enthusiastically by way of reply. Ray approached the shopkeeper, actually a young lad of scarcely more than their own age.

"Two of these, please!" he said.

The boy did not understand so Ray took the top off the jar and lifted out two doughnuts. The boy took out a piece of tissue paper and spread it on the board and Ray put the doughnuts down on the paper. Then he looked at the fruit and saw there was a tray of fresh dates. They were very big compared with the usual dried dates that are eaten in England. He took six out of the basket and put them beside the doughnuts. "How much?" he asked.

The boy serving thought for a moment and then said something which they could not understand. Ray took out some coins and held them out in his palm for the boy to take what was necessary, but the boy, after fingering one or two of the pennies and six-pences doubtfully, called across the street to a sort of carpenter's workshop.

In a few seconds a man came out wiping his hands on his apron, crossed the street and stared at the money in Ray's hands.

"Inglis money?" he inquired.

"It's all I have, I'm afraid," said Ray apologetically.

"Is no matter," said the man. He looked at the food on the paper and then at the money for some time; then, giving his hands an extra hard wipe, he took two more dates and put them with the six Ray had already chosen, and at the same time took a sixpence out of Ray's hand, holding it out first to make sure that they had all seen which coin it was.

"Is that all?" said Ray, surprised.

"Is okay," said the man, smiling. He gave the sixpence to the boy in the shop and then waved his hands at the doughnuts and dates as if telling Ray to clear them away.

"Well, thank you very much," said Ray, picking up the paper.

"Okay," said the man, already backing across the street to his work. "*Grazie!*"

"*Grazie!*" said the boy in the shop.

"That must mean thank you," said Ray. "*Grazie! Grazie* very much."

They went on, munching happily. The doughnuts were crisp and fresh and were almost a meal in themselves. The dates were rather woody in the center, but delicious in flavor. The street entered an open square where a street market was being held, and after the dimness of the little alley they were almost dazzled by the sudden riot of color. Stalls covered with flowers, with fruit, and with bright scarves and neckcloths broke up the darkness of the corners and made everything seem to glow. One man was selling large handkerchieves and, not having a stall to display them on, he had scattered them on a large sheet of brown paper laid on the ground. People stood around looking down at them, and as they were mostly bright blues and greens the muddle of handkerchieves looked at first glance like a pool of clear water that had suddenly bubbled up out of the grimy gray cobblestones.

Ray thought how nice it would be to have one; it could be worn around the throat the way cowboys do. Anti must have been thinking much the same for he picked out two very gay ones, blue with twiggy patterns, and offered the man a handful of money as Ray had done for the doughnuts. The man took a two-shilling piece and seemed well satisfied. Anti handed Ray one of the handkerchieves and began to knot the other around his own throat; it looked very dashing.

They were still admiring one another's appearance when a little lady in gray crossed the street toward them. She carried a gray silk parasol, wore white net gloves, and had a fussy little piece of veil hanging from her hat and over her eyes. There was something oddly old-fashioned about her, as if she had stepped out of an illustration in one of those old children's books that no one reads any more. She spoke to them in very clear English.

"Little boys!"

Ray didn't like this very much, but she was quite
an old lady and probably meant no harm by it.

"You look English," the lady went on.

"I'm English," said Ray. "Anti is from Finland."

"There now," said the lady and considered them
in turn, peeping from under her veil in sharp little
glances. "Well, I thought you might like to know
that if you go up there and turn right by the old
fountain you'll be in the oldest street in Naples."

"Thank you," said Ray politely. "I should think
all this is pretty old, though."

"Well, yes," said the lady. "But my street—I call it
my street because I live in the tall brown house on
the corner—no, you can't quite see it from here—my
street is quite the oldest. You must go and look."

She bobbed her head at them and walked on as if
satisfied. Ray did not care very much about the
oldest street in Naples, but he did not like to hurt
people's feelings, so nudging Anti he started off in
the direction she had indicated. Sure enough they
found an old fountain, not working and filled with
empty cigarette packets and bottles, and on the right
of it another narrow street, much like the others,
with high houses going up to five or six stories on
either side, and washing stretched on lines from the
balconies, and dirty cobblestones underfoot.

The boys were just wondering if it was worth the

trouble to walk up it when suddenly the rain started. It didn't begin with a few drops and then gradually increase in strength; it began at full strength right from the start, just as if someone had turned on a cold shower. The boys ran for the brown house on the corner and pressed themselves against a high gate that was set back a little in an archway so as to give a foot or two of shelter. Luckily there was no wind and the rain fell straight in front of them making a line in the dust just in front of their toes.

"This isn't very funny," said Ray, beginning to shiver. Both boys wore just shirts and shorts. Anti grinned and hugged himself.

The rain lasted quite a long time, or at least it seemed a long time. It must have been twenty minutes. The water gathered into a stream in the middle of the street and ran down the hill like a young torrent carrying bits of straw and paper, stale fruit and tomatoes and all the other rubbish along with it. Then, as suddenly as it had started, the rain stopped and the sun came out hard and bright and the street was clean and gleaming. The silence immediately after the shower was uncanny; it was if the whole city had gone into hiding until the rain had passed. Then into this silence there came the unmistakable sound of a ship's siren.

"The ship!" cried Ray. "What's the time?"

Neither of them had a watch and there were no public clocks in sight. The boys looked at each other with appalled expressions. What happened when ships were ready to leave? Did they wait for people? In any case no one knew they were ashore. As if thinking the same thing they jumped out of the gateway and bolted down the hill, going more or less the way they had come, but in any case making for the direction of the siren.

They blundered through puddles, leaped piles of rubbish, knocked into people and lost their way three times before they found their way down to the dock gates again. It seemed miles across the open space and they were both ready to drop by the time they reached the corner of the tourist bureau and swung round it on to the dock. It was empty.

"It must be the wrong place," Ray cried desperately.

But it wasn't. This was where the *Huron* had been tied up less than two hours ago, and now there was no sign of her at all. The shining metal gangways were drawn back against the side of the shed.

Ray stared out into the harbor, giving his eyes a hard rub to make sure of seeing properly. And right out, beyond the mouth of the harbor, was the familiar shape of the S.S. *Huron* making for the open sea.

9. No English spoken here

When Ray dragged his eyes away from the disappearing *Huron* he felt loneliness, helplessness and despair come down on him like a blanket. Usually when you were in some sort of fix there was something you could do, or someone you could turn to. But to whom could he turn here? People in the street would not even be able to understand him, let alone help him. And what did people do when they'd been left behind in a foreign country? He had a dreadful picture of himself and Anti wandering about the streets of Naples until their last few shillings had been spent and then dying of starvation in the gutter. No one would worry. No one knew about them. Even when Mrs. Wiley found out he was not there on the ship what could she do about it?

He turned to Anti and again felt annoyed that his friend could not understand English. It would have been a comfort to have someone to talk to.

"Oh, stop blubbering!" he said fiercely, for Anti

was, in fact, wiping his eyes on his sleeve. And Ray was too near to crying himself to feel any sympathy.

"Anti!" he exclaimed and gave the boy a shake. "Look, stop it, will you? We'll think of something. We'll find somebody who can help. We'll ask a policeman or something."

Anti could not possibly have understood all this, but he must have got the general idea, for he gave a gigantic sniff and then managed a rather wobbly grin.

"That's the stuff," said Ray, thinking at the same time how ridiculous it was that he should be looking after someone when he hardly felt able to look after himself. He wondered if leaders of famous expeditions sometimes felt like this, and only "pushed on with great determination," as the books said afterward, because they didn't want their followers to be disappointed in them.

"Let's push on with determination," he said aloud. "We must allow no obstacle to stand in our way. Forward, men!" He waved his arm at the impenetrable jungle of the empty pier and together the two boys faced the strange city.

Just at the end of the dock some buses had drawn up in a line and in front of them stood two or three men in uniform. They did not look like policemen, but there was no harm in trying. Ray went up to the nearest.

"Excuse me," he said, "but do you speak English?"

The man turned with a broad smile. "Much English," he said, and pointed to a large badge which he wore on his coat lapel. "Official guide. You go to Pompeii?"

"No, thank you," said Ray. "As a matter of fact we should have been on that ship that just sailed. The S.S. *Huron*. I was wondering if you could tell us what to do?"

"You left behind, eh?" said the man, looking serious. "That very sad thing, I think. You very naughty boys miss boat, eh?"

This wasn't a great deal of help. "What shall we do?" said Ray.

The man pushed back his peaked cap and

scratched his head. This seemed to bring inspiration, for he suddenly brightened up. "Have you try government tourist office?" he asked.

"No. Where is it?"

The man pointed to the large modern building right on the side of the dock. "In there," he said. "Easy find."

"Thank you very much," said Ray.

"Sank you muk," said Anti.

They all nodded at each other and the boys entered the wide central doors into a vast echoing hall. At the far end they could see a notice TOURIST BUREAU and they headed for it.

The tourist bureau seemed to consist of a large polished counter on which were displayed brightly colored pictures of the Bay of Naples, Vesuvius in eruption, the Ruins of Pompeii and so on. There was a large street plan of the city on the wall behind. Nobody seemed to be around. As there was a small handbell on the counter Ray picked it up and rang it.

Nothing happened for some seconds. Then a door opened at the back and a girl of about seventeen put her head around. She had a lipstick in one hand and was obviously in the middle of making up her face.

"Office closed," she said.

"This is very important . . ." Ray began.

"Sorry," said the girl, not prepared to argue. "To-

93

morrow morning. Nine o'clock." Then she disappeared and the door closed.

"That's that," said Ray and shrugged his shoulders. "All the same, we must be able to do something before tomorrow."

They went out into the open again. All the buses had disappeared and all the guides with them. The huge space between the docks and the dock gates was quite empty except for a rusty old shunting engine worrying about on the far side, and a little girl of eight or so playing some game in one of the large puddles left by the rain.

"I think we'd better try the police at the dock gates," Ray said. He had to talk to somebody, and even though Anti did not understand, at least he made sympathetic faces.

"Yes, that's a very good idea, old chap. I wish I'd thought of it myself," Ray answered himself.

"Well, what are we waiting for?" said Ray.

They went across the middle of the empty space. As they passed the little girl in the puddle she waved a hand at them and said, "Chow!" or something that sounded like that.

"Do you speak English by any chance?" said Ray.

The girl giggled and hid her face in both hands. As they walked on she shrieked something after them in Italian and splashed handfuls of water at them.

"Well, there's a policeman, anyway," Ray said, looking over toward the gate.

By this time the men outside the gate had all gone away and the policeman was alone. As Ray looked at him the policeman lit a cigarette and then, leaving it hanging from the corner of his mouth, he unbuttoned his revolver holster, took out his gun and started to examine it, blowing dust off it here and there and polishing parts of it on his sleeve. Somehow a policeman smoking and playing with a gun was not so reassuring. He no longer looked like the sort of person you went to for help and advice.

They walked more slowly as they approached the gate. The policeman aimed his revolver at a passing dog, squinting along the barrel and swinging the gun round as the dog trotted past. "Pfft!" he said suddenly, and shuffled his feet. The dog cringed and scurried away. The policeman laughed and returned his gun to its holster.

Maybe, thought Ray, they had committed some crime by getting left behind. Suppose they were arrested or something? After all, it was a crime to be a stowaway on a ship, and now they were sort of stowaways on land. Ray remembered a story the stewards had told him about a stowaway who had been put

95

ashore at Aden and imprisoned by the police, and when the ship returned they heard that the man had died in prison.

"You know," he said aloud, "I don't think it is such a bright idea to ask a policeman. Let's just walk past and have a look around the town. Something might turn up."

Anti didn't argue, so that was what they did. The policeman glared at them through the bars of the gate so that they were glad to hurry toward the open streets again.

This time it was quieter and there was nobody trying to sell them watches or sunglasses or pictures of Vesuvius—just a foreign city going about its ordinary business and not the slightest bit interested in two lost little boys. They went along the main street, but this time Ray was carefully reading all the signs and notices over shops and offices in the hopes of finding something that would give him an idea.

The shops were beginning to close, however, and people were coming out of the large office buildings with briefcases under their arms and cheerful looks on their faces that told they had finished work for the day and were on their way home. They were not likely to be much help. Two or three shops had notices in the windows saying that English was

96

spoken there, but in each case the doors were locked and the blinds down.

At the end of half an hour they had been down so many streets that Ray had lost count and had found nothing. By this time the main streets were getting empty and everything was closed. It was a waste of time to go on looking.

"I'm afraid it's tomorrow morning at the tourist office," Ray said. "At least we know they open at nine. The only thing is we'll have to find somewhere to sleep tonight." The idea made him shiver, for now that the sun had gone down it was not at all warm. "The question is, where?" he added.

Suddenly he remembered the urchins crowded round the bowl full of blazing sticks. "That's the way!" he exclaimed. "We'll have to find a place somewhere and light a fire. Wood, and matches, that's what we need!"

It was easier to get matches than wood. Some few stands selling papers and cigarettes on the edge of the pavement were still open and from one of these Ray bought a box of tiny wax matches, paying for them in the way he had found successful before; that is to say, holding out the money and letting the shopkeeper take what was right. This time the man took a shilling, which seemed a lot of money for a box of matches, but it was no use worrying.

Obviously there would not be much wood lying about in the main streets, so they wandered away from the lights and into the back streets and alleys, looking round corners and into dark places. Anti soon saw what Ray wanted and together they began to collect handfuls of rubbish.

"We need a base," said Ray. "We'll need a lot more than this if it's going to keep us warm all night."

They wandered from street to street and eventually found one which seemed to contain warehouses with open wasteland between them. They crept through a gap in a brokendown fence into a sort of yard where it was sheltered from the wind and where a fire would not attract too much attention. It had the faint smell of a rubbish dump about it, but it was not too strong to stand.

"This will do for a camp," Ray announced, putting down his load. "Now we must build up stocks."

They were lucky enough to find two empty wooden cases over against the shed wall and they soon broke these into useful lengths. A little farther away they found a brokendown cart and after struggling for a while they succeeded in pulling three or four heavy planks from its floor. Three of the wheels were quite firmly attached to the wreck, but one of them had fallen off on its own accord and was lying half-covered with weeds. Together they got it up and wheeled it slowly to their camp.

"That should do," said Ray, looking at the heap of firewood with pride. "Anyway, it's too dark to look around any more. Let's get a fire going!"

They built a small fire of paper, shavings, dried grass and sticks inside the old wheel. This was Anti's idea, and although he couldn't explain why, Ray saw that the heavy oak hub of the wheel would never burn unless it was warmed up for some time. When the small fire was going well they laid bits of broken box across the spokes of the wheel, and as these burned in the center and then fell into the fire it was hot enough to set fire to the ends of the more solid planks from the cart. Ray put three of these

99

so that the ends poked over the fire, his idea being that as they burned away they could be edged farther and farther in. This worked very well and soon the boys had a small but really warm fire going.

They crouched on either side of it and grinned at each other across the flames, and for the first time since they had seen the *Huron* halfway out of the harbor felt fairly happy.

But the night lasts a long time for those who don't sleep. In a warm bed the morning seems only a few moments later than the night before, but when you crouch over a fire in the open air with the bare sky above you and the cold wind on your back, then every

single minute of the night stretches its fullest length. Talking makes the time pass, but Ray and Anti could not talk because they could not understand each other.

After half an hour this thought struck Ray very forcibly. "I wish I could understand Finnish or you could understand English!" he exclaimed. Anti said something in Finnish which probably meant the same thing.

"We could sing," said Ray. "That's an idea. We could take it in turns to sing all the songs we knew. That would pass the time!"

He began to sing, rather shyly at first, but getting more confident as he went on. He sang a carol first— "Hark, the Herald Angels Sing." When he had finished he pointed to Anti, and the Finnish boy nodded and immediately began to sing a queer little song in his own queer-sounding language. And so they went on, taking turn and turn about for at least an hour.

At the end of this time they stopped, partly because their throats felt strained and stiff with so much singing, and partly because they had run out of songs. And an hour out of a whole night is really not long.

Then Ray had the brightest idea so far. If Anti did not understand English then the thing to do was to teach him! After all, he was going to Australia and everybody there spoke English, so he would have to learn sooner or later. Better to start learning now. And they had the whole night before them!

"Fire!" said Ray, pointing to it. And so the first lesson began.

"Dark," said Ray. "Sky, wood, earth, wheel."

And Anti repeated the words after him, obviously approving of the idea and eager to learn.

10. Ask a policeman

The long night dragged itself slowly over them. The stars wheeled; the air grew chill and poked icy fingers into the boys' backs. The city became quieter and quieter, and the distant street lamps seemed to have the glazed look that the eyes of a dead fish have. Now and then the sound of a solitary car starting up and changing from gear to gear seemed to make more noise than the whole of the traffic by day.

The boys drowsed and nodded over their fire. They could not lie down to sleep properly because the ground was cold; they could only sit crouched by the flames, nodding and jerking awake and nodding again. Now and again they had to jump to their feet, stamp and flap their arms to make sure to keep their muscles from being cramped.

Sometime before sunrise they ran out of wood for their fire and it was too dark to go searching around again. The fence they had crept through was in such a tumbledown state already that Ray thought a few more boards of it would not be missed. Together they managed to prise four of the rottenest away from the rusty nails, and these lasted them until daylight.

"First," Ray said. "Breakfast!"

Anti knew this word. "Yes pliz," he said immediately.

They crawled out of their camp and went back toward the more built-up part of the city. The streets were still empty and the sun was too low to throw any warmth between the houses, so the boys trotted for a while to keep warm. Then, flushed and breathless, they turned a corner and almost ran into their breakfast. A small milk float was standing in the street and a man and a boy were putting the cartons out on the steps.

"Pity we haven't got any cornflakes to go with it," Ray said, "but it will be better than nothing."

They asked the milkman in sign language for two cartons of milk. When the man lifted two out of his crate Ray held out his money. A blank look came over the man's face. He turned the money over with the tip of his finger as if it were made of some strange metal he'd never seen before, then he shook his head firmly and dropped the two milk containers back in his crate.

"English money," said Ray, giving his hand a little

104

shake. "Good money!" He picked out his last half-crown and offered it although he knew that it was more than the milk was worth.

But the man shook his head again and saying a great deal in Italian which Ray could not even guess the meaning of, he dug in his leather satchel and produced a handful of Italian coins and grubby, crumpled paper money to show Ray what he wanted.

"But I haven't any Italian money!" Ray said.

The milkman shrugged his shoulders as if to say that in that case he was very sorry but there was nothing he could do, and went on busily with his work. The float moved farther down the street and the boys stood in appalled silence, watching their breakfast being cleared away before they had even tasted it.

"We shall have to wait until the shops open," Ray said. "I don't want doughnuts for breakfast, but if that's all we can buy then it will have to do."

They turned away disappointed and had taken a few steps down the street when the boy helping the milkman ran after them and thrust a couple of containers of milk into their hands. Ray started to reach in his pocket for the money again, but the boy only laughed and ran off, and when they looked back to see what the milkman himself thought, there he was in the street waving at them in a friendly fashion,

trying to indicate that the milk was a gift from him.

"Thank you very much!" shouted Ray, holding up his carton, and then, remembering the one Italian word he had learned, added *"Grazie!"*

They drank the milk and felt much refreshed, and as they walked on in search of a garbage can Ray caught sight of a clock on a small tower in the direction of the harbor. Its hands showed ten minutes to nine.

"Time for the tourist bureau," Ray announced, and they walked along the now familiar streets toward the gates of the dock. "We'll wait outside the office until it opens and then we'll be sure to be the first," he said.

They crossed the open streets and approached the gates. The policeman on the other side was standing with his back to them staring dreamily out to the distant sea and at a liner that was just entering the port.

Anti pointed excitedly. "Ship!" he said. *"Ooron!"*

For a moment Ray thought so too. It was ridiculous, of course, to imagine that the *Huron* would have returned for them after being at sea all night. But it was the same shade of pale brown, it had the same markings on the funnel, and it looked the same shape. Or almost the same.

"No," said Ray. "It isn't the *Huron,* although it must be a sort of sister ship. It might be the *Cheyenne* or the *Sioux,* although I think the *Cheyenne* is supposed to be on the way back from Australia." All this was stewards' gossip which Ray had picked up below decks. Frank had served on all three ships, and from the conversation Ray knew that the *Sioux* was the newest of the three, and although slightly smaller than the *Huron* was much faster, and did the trip to Australia in five or six days' less time.

However, that wasn't getting them through the gate. Ray caught hold of the bars, shook them and gave a polite cough. The policeman turned slowly as if on a string and stared solemnly at the boys, but he did not make any move to open the gate.

"Can we come through?" Ray asked, with a smile.

The policeman looked up at the sky as if dredging in the depths of his memory for some slight knowledge of English. He dug out two words, "Pass, please!"

Ray thought at first he meant they must pass the gate, then he realized he wanted to see their passes.

"We haven't got a pass," Ray said. "We want to go to the tourist bureau."

The policeman shook his head ponderously. "No pass, no come," he announced. He took a piece of plywood down from the wall and showed it to them, pointing to where he thought they should read. Some official regulations in Italian were pasted to the board.

"We don't understand Italian," Ray said.

The policeman looked at the board himself and read the item over. Then he said, "Here she is writing no one must come through door when she have no pass."

"But you see," explained Ray, beginning to feel desperate, "we were on the *Huron* . . ."

"S.S. *Huron?*" said the policeman, showing interest.

"Yes. We are passengers. Going to Australia."

The policeman's eyes gleamed. "You passengers on *Huron?*" he insisted.

"Yes," said Ray. "I'm trying to tell you."

"You are much big liar," said the policeman with great satisfaction. "S.S. *Huron* she sail yesterday."

"I know she sailed," cried Ray. "And we got left behind."

The policeman shook his head as if to say Ray would have to think up a much better story than that to convince him. "I know boys," he said. "You want for be stowaway. All boys want for be stowaway." He shook a plump finger at them. "Bad boys! Now must run home to momma. Bad boys run for stowaway make momma cry. Go away home! Shoo!"

Ray turned to Anti. "It's no use," he cried. "I can't make him understand."

"Me understand plenty," shouted the policeman through the gate. "Go home! Shoo! Shoo!"

It was useless to stay at the gate any longer and they moved away. Ray sat down on the edge of the pavement and put his head in his hands. He had tried hard to be brave and sensible, and he had really thought all their troubles would be solved once they got back to the tourist bureau. Now to be prevented when they could actually see the place through the gate was too much for him, and the tears began to trickle through his fingers and drip into the dust in the gutter. He saw the tears and tried angrily to stop them by squeezing his fingers tightly against his eyes, but it was no use; they had been held back too long.

Anti tugged at his sleeve, but Ray shook him off. He did not want the Finnish boy to look at him while he was in this state. "I'm all right," he muttered. "Just leave me alone, can't you?"

"Ray!" said Anti. "Come! Pliz! I show!"

Ray took no notice. What could Anti show him? He didn't realize the trouble they were in. He was used to being surrounded by people speaking languages he could not understand; he did not realize that this was different.

"Ray! Come!" said Anti, and his voice was so urgent that Ray looked up, forgetting the tearmarks he had been hoping to hide.

"What's eating you now?" he said in a rough sort of voice, trying to cover up his babyishness in crying.

"Yes. You come. Ray come Anti."

"All right," said Ray, getting to his feet. "If it

gives you any pleasure. It doesn't really matter where
we go, I suppose. It's no good staying here, anyway."

Having once got Ray on the move, Anti led him
along at a trot. Ray noticed it was the same way they
had gone the day before, and could not imagine what
Anti had in his mind. Then he remembered that this
was where the doughnut shop had been.

"Doughnuts!" he said to Anti.

Anti grinned and went on.

"Oh, well, a pint of milk wasn't much of a break-fast," said Ray. "And I did say . . . here, wait a minute, old chap. You've run right past it in your hurry!"

But Anti shook his head and made a fierce face when Ray tried to go inside the little shop where they had bought doughnuts and dates. "No eat!" he said. "Come Anti."

Now Ray was really mystified and followed round the next two or three corners blindly.

Anti grabbed his sleeve and pointed across the narrow street. "Here!" he cried triumphantly. "See? Lady!" And his finger was pointing at the brown house where they had taken shelter from the rain, and where the odd little English lady had said she lived. Ray suddenly awakened to what Anti was after.

"Anti," he cried, "you're a genius! Why didn't I think of her myself?"

And with that they ran across the entrance to the oldest street in Naples and began to beat loudly on the high wooden gate.

11. Very nars lady

The odd little English lady was delighted to see them and after hearing their story threw up her hands in horror.

"All night in the open by yourselves!" she exclaimed. "If only I'd known. Why didn't you think of coming to me right away? But never mind, you got here in the end. Are you hungry?"

They were, and said so. In twenty minutes, after a good wash, they were sitting up to a table on which was set out enough breakfast for six people.

"There's more if you need it," she said. "Now you start in on it while I go and get busy on the telephone and straighten all this trouble out for you."

So the boys ate and looked around them, while from the next room came the tinging of the telephone and the lady's voice talking to a large number of people in what sounded like very voluble Italian.

The table had been laid on a sort of veranda that was really like a room with one side open to the air.

The floor was mosaic with interesting pictures worked in small stones. Beyond the stone parapet was the garden with a sprinkler hose showering sparkling drops on a small lawn, and a small stone fountain in the shape of a dolphin throwing up a double jet of water into the sunlight. The house, in fact, was built back-to-front. Its only doors opened on the garden and the few windows opening on to the street were all covered with heavy wooden shutters. The garden was small but neat and had just room for three trees, one of them an orange tree with the small ripe fruit still on the boughs.

Before they had finished their breakfast the lady came back with a look of triumph on her face. "Well," she said, "I've talked to a lot of stupid people who all tried to make difficulties, but they came round in the end."

"What's going to happen to us?" Ray asked. "Has there been any fuss about our missing the ship?"

"Has there been a fuss? I'll say there has. The shipping office had a cable from the *Huron* telling them to search for you, and they've had men out on the job pretty well all night. I must say you tucked yourself and your little campfire away very cleverly. Still, don't let's worry about all that now that we know you're safe. I persuaded the shipping office to cable to the *Huron* telling your people that you'd been found, and arranging for you to travel on the next boat."

"The next boat! All by ourselves?" said Ray.

"As far as that goes, you're in luck. The S.S. *Sioux* has just come in and will be sailing again at six this evening. She's a faster boat than your *Huron,* and with any luck you should catch up and be back with your people by the time you reach Aden."

"That's wonderful," said Ray. "I've heard about the *Sioux,* and she's supposed to be the best ship on the Australian run."

The lady smiled. "Well, don't count your chickens before they're hatched," she said. "We've still to wait and see if the arrangements can be made. Meanwhile, you're my guests for the day. Have you finished your breakfast yet?"

"I think I could manage another peach," said Ray.

"Then have it, dear."

There was a queer sound from outside, a sound halfway between a cock crowing and a loud hiccup.

"That's the car," the lady said. "Perhaps you'd better put the peach in your pocket and come along now. Alberto hates to be kept waiting; he says it wastes gas. Are you ready?"

"Ready for what?" asked Ray.

"I thought we'd have a little drive out into the country, round the Bay perhaps, and get some lunch

on the way, and then be back in time for the ship. And we mustn't let you miss it this time."

She led the way out through the garden and through the gate to where the car was waiting in the street, ticking over silently. Ray stopped short at the gate and stared.

"It's a Rolls Royce!" he said.

"A very old one," said the lady apologetically. "A 1928 model. But it is rather sweet, isn't it? And I've had it so long that I can't bear to part with it now."

"Sweet!" exclaimed Ray. "It's a knock-down smasher. It's a . . . *beaut!*"

"That's an Australian expression, isn't it?" said the lady with a smile. Ray blushed. He was always telling Ila it sounded silly, and here he was using it himself.

But the Rolls *was* a beaut for all that. Every inch of it shone in the sunlight. The old-fashioned square lines, the wide running boards and steering column almost upright gave the car such a look of dignity that Ray found himself holding the door open for the lady and then bowing slightly as she passed him.

They settled themselves on the worn but richly up-holstered seat and the lady unhooked the micro-phone and spoke to the chauffeur in Italian. Through the glass partition they saw him nod gravely and then the car glided gently forward.

The ride was a delight for both boys, not only on account of the car, but because they drove through vineyards and orange orchards and went up to the very slopes of Vesuvius. Mrs. MacLaren, for that was the lady's name, had Alberto stop the car so that the boys could get out and scramble about on the cold, gray lava at the foot of the mountain. Both boys found pieces small enough to go into their pockets for souvenirs.

"It's pumice stone, you know," the lady told them. "You can use it for getting ink off your fingers when you start school again."

"Don't spoil our day by talking of school," said Ray.

They had lunch in the open air on the veranda of a very expensive sort of restaurant and drove back to-ward Naples by the road along the edge of the sea.

"All that sea and sand," said Ray. "If only we'd brought our bathing trunks . . ."

Mrs. MacLaren smiled and picked up the micro-phone. Alberto did not take his eyes off the road as he listened, but when she had finished he put his left hand down on the seat beside him and picked up two pairs of bright red swimming trunks that had been lying there out of sight.

"You think of everything," Ray said. "Can we really have a swim?"

"Of course," said Mrs. MacLaren. "I shall enjoy watching you."

So the car stopped once again near a small, empty beach, and the two boys had their swim. And afterward, when they returned to Mrs. MacLaren's house, there was a splendid tea waiting for them, and after the tea the Rolls was brought round once more to take them down to the docks to go on board the S.S. *Sioux*. It was the end of a perfect day, and Ray said so.

"Don't thank me," said Mrs. MacLaren. "I'm sure I'm the one who has enjoyed it most. I live a very quiet life usually. But I do hope you get on all right in Australia. I'm sure you will; you're both just the right independent sort."

Ray hesitated and then said, "Would you let me write to you when we get there—just to let you know we're all right? You don't need to answer, of course . . ."

"I'd love you to write," said Mrs. MacLaren. "And I shall certainly answer. It will be nice to have a friend right over on the other side of the world."

Ray had been thinking this too, but he didn't

know how to put it into words, so he said nothing. He and Anti stood at the top of the gangway and watched the Rolls drive gently across the open space toward the dock gates. They noticed that the policeman saluted as the car passed through and then it was lost in the busy Naples traffic. The boys sighed and turned to the steward who was waiting to show them to their cabin.

"Well, that was a day," said Ray.

Anti said slowly, "Very—nars—lady!"

"Nice," said Ray.

Anti nodded. "Nars," he repeated.

"It's time you had some more lessons in English," said Ray.

12. Diving for spoons

The S.S. *Sioux* was all they expected her to be. Everything on board was brand new and a delight to look at. She rolled less and traveled faster than the old *Huron,* the cabins were more comfortable, there were armchairs in the salon, and the swimming pool was almost twice the size. She caught up with the *Huron* in time to go through the Suez Canal in the same convoy, but the boys were not transferred until both ships were in Aden.

Anti disappeared into the arms of his mother and his family amid a positive torrent of Finnish; Ray was warmly received by Mrs. Wiley, who had been worried but had had time to get over it, knowing that Ray was safe on the *Sioux.* Ila's welcome was a little cooler, but even she seemed pleased to see Ray safe. For some days Ray was stopped by passengers he had never noticed before and asked how he had got on during his day adrift at Naples. Frank and the other stewards on H deck held a little party in honor of both boys and gave them cream cakes, ice cream and pineapple slices which had been scrounged from the galley by Studs. On the whole Ray was surprised to find himself so well known.

Ray gave Anti English lessons every day for an hour or more, and when Anti asked if his younger sister Serpa could learn as well Ray found he was starting a little class which grew to six children by the time they reached Colombo. By this time Anti knew quite a lot of English and was able to use it around ship, so that Ray felt quite proud of his efforts.

"And it all started because we had to stay awake one night," he said.

After Colombo they had the long voyage across uninterrupted sea for nine days when, apart from the flying fish and a very distant whale, there was nothing at all to see. Everyone who had made the trip before had said this was the worst part because the passengers got so bored, but for Ray it was, apart from the day in Naples, the best part of the whole trip.

In the first place there was the ceremony of Crossing the Line when King Neptune—really a sailor dressed up—came aboard. With the other children who had not crossed the equator before Ray was smothered with ice cream and ducked in the swimming pool before being given his certificate. This was fun enough, but better still were the swimming sports which took the whole of one baking-hot afternoon.

As the boys lined up to give their names in for the events Ray noticed Andrew Newman three or four places ahead of them in the line and suddenly remembered the feud they'd had at the beginning of the voyage. It seemed ages ago now. But revenge was revenge. Ray nudged Anti and nodded forward at Andrew's back. "Don't forget," he said. "Enter for everything."

Anti looked puzzled for a moment and then he too remembered and grinned with delight. "You think we win him?" he asked.

"Beat him," said Ray. "Sure we will." They shook hands on it.

But beating Andrew was not very easy. He was heavy for his age and had no difficulty in winning the events where weight was important, such as the pillow fight on the pole. By the time the last event was called the score was Andrew twelve points, Ray and Anti thirteen each. This meant that Andrew could not beat them if they lost in the spoon diving contest, which was the last event, but that he could tie for first place.

"We must both beat him," Ray said. "We've got

to make him come third. It doesn't matter which of us comes first as long as the other one comes second, see?" Anti appeared to understand.

There were twelve or thirteen boys entered for the event, so they dived in twos for a start to see which one of each couple could get most of the forty spoons thrown into the pool. Ray and Anti and Andrew all qualified for a second dive and they were to go one at a time. Andrew was called first.

"Can't we have more than forty spoons?" he cried. "In the men's event they had sixty."

The people crowded round the pool groaned aloud at this, but it was the sort of thing Andrew might have been expected to say, so the judge didn't answer but merely cried out, "Prepare to dive! Dive!"

Andrew went in neatly and was seen to be swimming methodically right round the pool picking up the spoons as he went.

"I bet the nasty fellow gets the lot," said one man bitterly.

Ray felt a hollow ache in his stomach and wished angrily to himself that he wasn't quite so set on winning. "After all," he thought, "it's only a game. It doesn't really matter."

Andrew came to the surface with both hands full of spoons and there was faint clapping. But when the spoons were counted it was found he had thirty-five.

"You must have counted wrong," he cried, and insisted on counting them himself. When it still came to thirty-five he began to peer suspiciously into the pool. "I don't think they were all thrown in," he declared.

Once again the judge ignored him and nodded at Anti to be the next. The spoons were dropped back into the water, and on the signal Anti followed them.

Anti was a poor diver and made such a splash that the judge was soaked. Nevertheless, he was very good under water. He went backward and forward across the pool four or five times and stayed down much longer than Andrew. When he came up very red in the face he got a tremendous cheer from the crowd.

"Thirty-nine!" cried the sailor who was counting.

The cheering burst out again. Ray swallowed hard. He would have to get every one of them to win now, and that was almost impossible. He grinned across the pool at Anti and then shook his fist in pretended annoyance.

"Prepare to dive! Dive!" called the judge.

Ray didn't take a deep breath, because he knew you could keep on the bottom more easily if you didn't fill your lungs with air. He dived for the middle of the pool first and picked up the half-dozen spoons there, then swam for the side and began to go around. The spoons shone out well in the sunlight,

each one like a bright star. It seemed impossible to miss any. He went right round picking up every spoon he saw until he was back at the same point again. He must have them all, he thought. However, he still had a little breath left so he started to swim round a second time to make sure. Almost immediately he found a spoon right against the side of the pool, out of the sunlight so that it did not shine. And just before his breath gave out he saw yet another. He came up with a rush to the surface, nearly bursting, and the sound of the applause broke over his head like thunder.

Ray came up the steps on the side of the pool away from the sailor, and as the man came around to count the spoons the judge stopped him and started to say something quietly in his ear. Ray put the spoons down on the deck and counted them himself while he was waiting.

He looked across the pool to where Anti was watching, his face a little strained. But he smiled quickly at Ray. Ray thought of the night they'd spent together, lonely and lost in a strange city. He heard a voice behind him in the crowd—an Australian voice —saying, "Those two kids will make dinkum Aussies."

The sailor came round and Ray moved away from the pile of spoons. There was absolute quiet as he counted. He counted twice.

"Thirty-nine!" he called out.

The applause was fantastic, people shouted and clapped, and it seemed as if they would never stop. Ray had no idea they were so popular.

The judge called for silence. "Would you like to dive again?" he said. "We'll put more spoons in if you like."

Ray looked across at Anti and both boys shook their heads at the same time. They were both well satisfied to share the honors.

As Ray turned away to go to the dressing room, he stopped and looked at the pool. Then he went down the steps into the water as if to cool off quickly. Once under the surface he slipped the fortieth spoon from under the belt of his trunks and let it drop to the bottom. Then he came out and he and Anti went into the shower together, laughing and scuffling.

A little later that day Mrs. Wiley came down to

the cabin and found Ray poking around in the top drawer. "Congratulations, Ray," she said. "I was ever so proud of you . . . what are you looking for?"

Ray looked a little embarrassed. "It was that letter from Aunt Netta," he said. "I thought perhaps I'd see what she said and write back to her. I could mail it from Perth, couldn't I?"

Mrs. Wiley looked surprised. "I think that would be a very good idea," she said. "But I thought you said . . ."

Ray twiddled the knob on the drawer. "Oh, a fellow can change his mind," he said. "Hobart doesn't sound like such a bad place."

Ila burst into the cabin. "Good on yer, Ray," she said. "You showed 'em!"

Ray smiled. Good on yer! It didn't seem such a silly way of talking after all. In fact, he quite liked it.